30 Hats in 30 Days

30 Hats in 30 Days
ISBN 13 (print): 978-1-937513-00-9
First edition
Published by http://www.cooperativepress.com

Patterns, charts ©2019 Marie Duquette
Photos ©2019 Tamas Jakab, Laura Wimbels, Marie Duquette
Models: Amelia Candelaria, Arabella Proffer, Camilla Grigsby, Ben
Szporluk, Christine Gallowan, Cimone Alyse, Mandy Lynn, Rhiannon
Blahnik, Dan Houseman, Qusae Farunia, Laura Wimbels

Technical Editor: Andi Smith
Book layout: Shannon Okey

Every effort has been made to ensure that all the information in this book is accurate at the time of publication; however, Cooperative Press neither endorses nor guarantees the content of external links referenced in this book.

If you have questions or comments about this book, or need information about licensing, custom editions, special sales, or academic/ corporate purchases, please contact Cooperative Press: info@cooperativepress.com or 10252 Berea Rd, Cleveland, Ohio 44102 USA

30 Hats in
30 Days

Cooperative Press
Cleveland, Ohio

For Charlie,
who supports me in all that I do,
not only in my knitting.

Patterns

Trøndelag, 16

Selbu Star, 20

Wind and Stars, 24

Selbu Star Redux, 28

Trøndelag at Night, 32

Rose Mandala, 36

Chorus Girl, 40

Prim Check and Ribbon, 44

Miter Box, 48

Pythagorean Band Beret, 52

Do-Si-Do, 56

Big Top Stocking Cap, 60

Slanted Columns, 64

Couldn't Be Easier, 68

Slam Hat, 72

Latvian Cloche, 76

Nordic Shimmer, 80

Weird Warm Hat, 88

Winter Stars, 92

Fancy Hug Beanie, 96

Stop the Purl, 100

Wood Stove Beanie, 104

Capitol Square, 108

Equine Cloche, 112

And Toto Too?, 116

Eastern Light, 120

Electric Cloche, 124

Sweet Peerie, 128

Eastern Diamonds, 134

Le Plat, 138

8

Intro

And so it began. It was early winter. I was recently retired. This was a new experience for me because I had always had somewhere to be in the morning. Now, I was faced with unstructured time. How would I fare? One November Sunday afternoon, I took a knitting class on traditional Scandinavian stranded knitting designs and I started knitting a sample hat in class. I hadn't knit a hat in years and this was so much fun! Later that same evening, I finished the hat while watching football and then the idea struck. Here's my original blog post:

November 14

Every once in a while, I get an idea. Here's the most recent one: Knit 30 hats in 30 days.

Most people would ignore this idea. A few might wonder why someone would want to do this. I can only speak for myself, so if you're still with me...

- I need to accomplish something tangible every day.
- I want to see if I can do it.
- I think it will be fun. And it will be fun to hear what other people think about my hats.
- It's cold so we're watching way too much football and old movies.
- 'Tis the season to be knitting hats.

I had so much fun knitting a hat in Mary Jane Mucklestone's Scandinavian Colorwork class, that I finished it that evening. It only took a few hours to knit and I didn't know that I could knit a hat in a day. Why not knit a hat every day? Well let's not get carried away.

So here we go!

- Starting November 15, I will knit a total of 30 hats through December 14.
- The hat can be any size.

- It must be my own design but I can use designs that I've knitted before.
- I must use yarn that I already have. I'll use yarns that are commercially available, although I can't promise that the color way will still be available.
- I will write down the pattern. This will be the most difficult part. Ugh.
- I will post a picture of the completed each day here, and also on Facebook, Twitter, and Instagram. On the blog and Facebook, I'll include information about yarn and gauge. There may also be a blurb on my inspiration, or musings on the process, or a recipe that I'm cooking for dinner...

Off to organize! Hope you cheer me on!

Thoughts on Knitting Hats

I've been knitting since childhood but I rarely knitted hats. Why? Because I was afraid that I couldn't knit a hat that would fit someone in particular. People are funny about what they put on their heads. A hat can be deemed unacceptable for very personal reasons. It may be too short, too long, too tight, too loose, too warm, too itchy, etc. But how can this be when commercially manufactured hats are sold by the millions and people seem to be happily wearing them everywhere?

However, I learned so much knitting so many hats so quickly. I became more confident in my knitting and designing skills. Even though it was challenging, it was fun! It was especially fun when I stopped worrying so much about fit, and it was so pleasing to use techniques that I had learned from other knitting projects as design elements.

After knitting 30 hats and showing them to a variety of people, I learned that each hat fit all sorts of heads in all sorts of sizes. It seems I am overly concerned about the fit when I'm knitting for someone specific. Perhaps you are too. So let's get started.

Size

I designed the hats in this book for very cold Wisconsin winters. They are meant to fit across the forehead at just above the eyebrows, to cover the ears completely, to reach the neck and to have some air space at the crown to capture the heat escaping from the head. Yes, in very cold climates, we think about these things.

When determining the size of the hat you want to knit, you need to know the circumference of the hat, the length of the hat from the bottom to the start of the crown shaping and the total length of the hat from the bottom to the top.

Size				
XS	S	M	L	1X
Typical Age				
9 months to toddler	Toddler	Child/Teen Small adult	Adult	Large adult
Circumference				
15.75 - 16.75 in 40 - 43.25 cm	17 - 19 in 43.25 - 48.25 cm	19 - 21 in 48.25 - 53.25 cm	21 - 23 in 53.25 - 58.5 cm	23 - 25 in 58.5 63.5 cm
Length to Crown				
4 - 5 in 10 - 12.75 cm	5 - 6 in 12.77 - 15.25 cm	5 - 6 in 12.77 - 15.25 cm	5 - 7 in 12.75 - 17.75 cm	6 - 7 in 5.25 - 17.75 cm
Total Length				
6 - 7 in 15.25 - 17.75 cm	6 - 7 in 15.25 - 17.75 cm	7 - 8 in 17.75 - 20.25 cm	8 - 9 in 20.25 - 23 cm	8 - 9 in 20.25 - 23 cm

*Hat circumference assumes 0.75 - 1 inch / 2 - 2.5 cm of negative ease from head measurement.

The hats in this book were designed to slouch, so the lengths vary and are usually longer than the typical length measurements.

Altering the Length

If you'd like to alter the length of the hat you are knitting, the pattern designates a place where you can either eliminate or add rounds to achieve the length you require before starting the crown shaping. Crown shaping usually takes up 1.5 - 3 inches / 3.75 - 7 cm of knitting to complete but it is a good idea to check your row or rnd gauge against the pattern to see how long your crown will be.

Number of rows / rnds in crown shaping : number of rows / rnds per inch / cm = length of crown

Gauge

When knitting a hat, it is very important to have the stitch gauge correct so that the hat will be the circumference that you want. It is sometimes difficult to get the same stitch gauge and row / rnd gauge as the designer. If this happens, use the stitch gauge and adjust the length of the hat as you knit by working fewer or more rows / rnds. See the notes above about altering the length.

Casting On

I used the long tail cast on for the hats in this book. It's a very popular method of casting on as it is firm yet stretchy. It is not quite as stretchy as the German Twisted cast on and not as firm as the cable cast on. Hats need a band that will hold up well when frequently being put on and taken off and the Long Tail Cast On Method fits the bill.

Needles

I used 24 inch interchangeable acrylic needles to knit these hats. This length worked for all sizes except XS and S. I used sticky wool so I preferred a slippery needle. If you're using slippery material, you might prefer to use wooden needles that grip the sts.

I used wooden dpns when I got to the crown shaping because of their extra grippiness. You could also use the Magic Loop method to knit the entire hat.

Use whatever length and type of needle that works best for you. I have large hands so a 16 inch circular and shorter needles are uncomfortable for me. I also prefer to use dpns rather than using the

Magic Loop method when knitting the crown. Recently, I discovered that I enjoy Magic Loop when I use a 32 inch circular needle rather than a longer needle.

My advice is to experiment with different needles to find the length and method that works best for you. Use what makes you happy and makes your knitting enjoyable.

Materials
All the hats in this book were knitted using wool or a wool blend yarn. When substituting yarn, look for a soft, airy yarn that will trap heat and is soft against the skin. Wool and wool blends are also springy and retain their shape. If you prefer cotton, silk, or alpaca, choose a yarn that is blended with either wool or acrylic for that springy quality. Pure cotton, silk or alpaca will likely stretch and grow in most of these designs.

It's also very important to get the pattern gauge with any yarn that with which you plan to work. Whether you are using the suggested yarn or a substitute, always swatch. Swatching not only gives you the opportunity to check your gauge but also lets you know if you're going to like the fabric you are creating. You can then decide if you like this fabric for your hat.

Remember that your gauge may differ significantly if you're knitting in the round rather than knitting flat (back and forth). Refer to the pattern to see which method was used and swatch accordingly.

Skills Required
Most of the hat patterns require basic knitting skills. Some employ skills that an adventurous beginner can master. Hats are a great way to boost your knitting skills because they are small projects and are usually knit at a medium gauge.

You can learn specific new skills through knitty.com and YouTube tutorials. Knitting classes and informal knitting groups are also great places for learning. When learning a new technique, remember to learn how to execute it when knitting in the round and when knitting flat (back and forth).

Blocking and Finishing

I steamed each hat using a hand held steamer and let each dry completely flat. I prefer to steam block when using 100% wool because it sets the stitches and turns the knitting into a cohesive fabric rather than a mesh of stitches. It also helps even out the tension in stranded work. If using a fiber other than wool, including Superwash wool, follow the yarn manufacturer's instructions. Generally a good soak and then lying flat to dry completely is a safe alternative to steam.

To reduce the itchiness of 100% wool, give the hat a good soak in water with hair conditioner or a commercial wool wash. Fill a basin with warm water and add a good squirt of hair conditioner or wool wash. Swish the water around to dissolve. When the water is room temperature, add the hat and squeeze the water through. Don't twist, wring or hang. Let the hat soak for a few hours. Rinse the hat in cool water unless the wool wash recommends otherwise. Squeeze out excess water and lay flat to dry. Once it is completely dry, give it a light steaming if you like.

Tips

- When knitting for a specific person, it's easier to measure a favorite hat than to measure a head.
- If you find the Magic Loop method cumbersome, try using a 32 inch needle rather than a 40 inch so there isn't as much cable interfering with your knitting or touching your thumbs and wrists as you knit.
- When knitting in the round with interchangeable circular needles and changing from smaller to larger needles, only change the working needle to the larger size. A smaller needle holding the sts makes it easier and quicker to knit with the larger needle.

Making tassels
Materials
Cardboard
Yarn
Tapestry needle

Cut a piece of sturdy cardboard into a 2 inch/ 5 cm by 4 inch/ 10 cm rectangle.

Cut a 12 inch/ 30 cm piece of yarn, thread a tapestry needle and set aside.

Wrap yarn around the length of the cardboard 20 times or so. You can make the tassel slimmer or fatter depending on your preference.

Using the yarn that was set aside, thread the yarn underneath all the tassel yarn at the top of the cardboard. Pull until there is an equal length of yarn on either side of the tassel yarn. Remove the tapestry needle. Tie the two ends snugly against the top of the tassel.

Cut the tassel yarn at the bottom of the cardboard. Remove the cardboard.

Cut a 12 inch/ 30 cm piece of yarn and wrap it snugly around the tassel, about 0.5 inch / 1.5 cm from the top. Tie a knot in the wrapped yarn ends and bury the ends inside the tassel.

Attach to the top of the hat by drawing the top ends of the tassel ends separately into the hat. The ends should be close together but not in the same hole. Tie the ends into a knot. Thread the ends and other nearby loose ends back to the outside of the hat. Bury all ends in the tassel.

Trim the tassel ends.

Trøndelag

The color pattern on this hat is a traditional pattern from the Trondelag region of Norway. Traditionally, it is worked with highly contrasting solid colors but the pattern is equally pleasing when knit with a solid and a hand-painted yarn. The top is shaped by using an ssk (left-leaning decrease) at the end of each pattern repeat on every other round. The result is dazzling. A 2x2 ribbing at the beginning is tucked into the hat to warm the ears.

Sizes
S (M, L, 1X)

Finished Measurements
Circumference 17.5 (19.75, 21.75, 23.25) inches / 44.5 (49.5, 55.25, 59) cm

Height to crown 7.25 (9, 9, 9) inches / 18.5 (22.75, 22.75, 22.75) cm

Total height 10.25 (12.25, 12.25, 12.25) inches / 26 (31.25, 31.25, 31.25) cm

Materials
Blackberry Ridge Woolen Mill Sport Weight Natural Colored Wool (100% wool; 350 yds per 4 oz skein); MC color: Cream; 1 skein

Blackberry Ridge Woolen Mill Sport Weight Kaleidoscope Yarn (100% wool; 180 yds per 2 oz skein); CC color: Ivory Coast; 1 skein

US#6 / 4mm circular needles, configured for small circumference knitting or size needed to obtain gauge

US#4 / 3.5mm circular needles, configured for small circumference knitting

1 set US#6 / 4mm double-point needles, two circulars, or one long circular for magic loop, as your prefer for knitting in the round over a small circumference

Stitch markers

Large-eyed sewing needle

Gauge
22 sts and 28 rounds = 4 inches / 10 cm in pattern stitch, on larger needles

Pattern
With smaller needles and MC, cast on 96 (108, 120, 132) sts. Being careful not to twist, join to work in the round. Place marker at start of rnd.

Rnd 1: *K2, p2; repeat from * to

end of rnd.

Repeat Rnd 1 for 20 rounds total.

Rnd 21: Purl.

Change to larger needles.

Rnd 22: Purl.

Join CC and work 14 rnds of Trøndelag main chart, 8 (9, 10, 11) times around.

Work 2 (3, 3, 3, 3) full repeats of Rnds 1 - 14, or to desired length before crown. Please note that ending after a partial chart repeat will mean that the crown chart will not line up. If you're comfortable with the pattern however, it is quite easy to continue in pattern as set, working the decreases in the places set in the crown chart.

Work 21 rnds of Trøndelag crown chart, working ssk decreases in the color indicated on the chart. Break yarn, leaving a 12 inch / 30.5 cm tail. Thread the yarn needle with the tail, and work through the remaining sts. Pull taut to close the top of the hat, and weave in ends.

Finishing

Fold ribbing into the inside of the hat, using the purl ridge as a guide. Loosely tack ribbing to inside of hat.

Block.

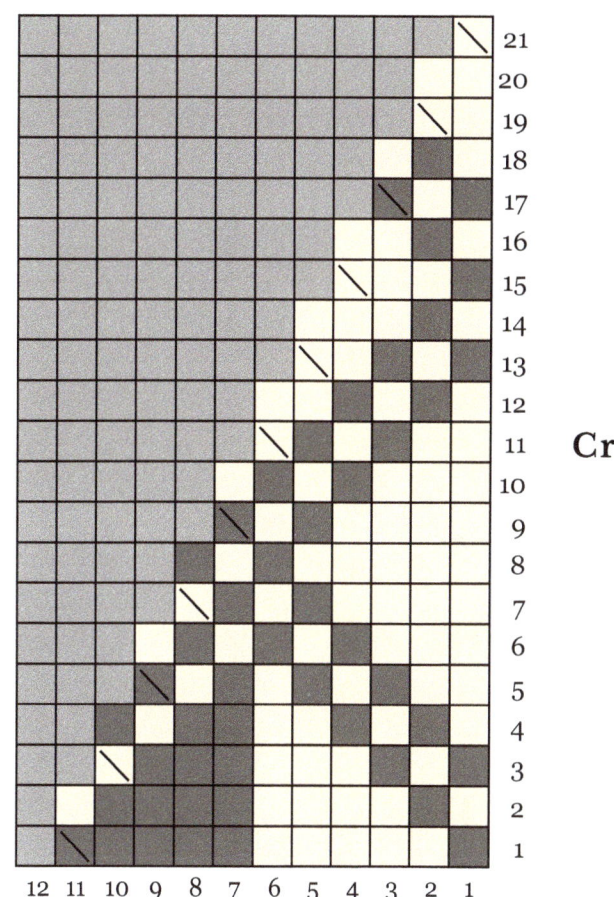

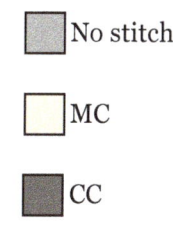

	No stitch
	MC
	CC
⟍	Ssk

Crown Chart

21
20
19
18
17
16
15
14
13
12
11
10
9
8
7
6
5
4
3
2
1

12 11 10 9 8 7 6 5 4 3 2 1

Body Chart

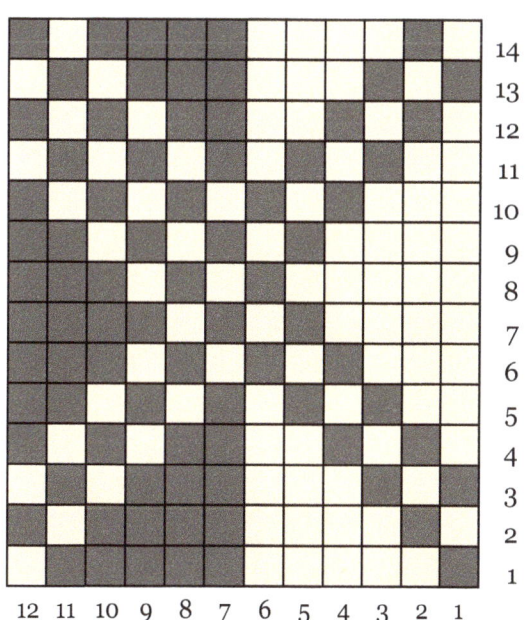

14
13
12
11
10
9
8
7
6
5
4
3
2
1

12 11 10 9 8 7 6 5 4 3 2 1

Selbu Star

The Selbu Rose or Star from the Selbu region of Norway is a very popular color pattern. Traditionally, the pattern is knit in solid colors. For a modern take, a natural contrasting yarn is paired with a hand-painted yarn. A double decrease at four points shapes the top.

Sizes
M (L, 1X)

Finished Measurements

Circumference 20.25 (21.75, 24) inches / 51.5 (55.25, 61) cm

Height to crown 7.5 inches / 19 cm

Total height 10.25 inches / 26 cm

Materials
Blackberry Ridge Woolen Mill Sport Weight Natural Colored Wool (100% wool; 350 yds per 4 oz skein); MC color: Cream; 1 skein

Blackberry Ridge Woolen Mill Sport Weight Kaleidoscope Yarn (100% wool; 180 yds per 2 oz skein); CC color: Blackberry; 1 skein

US#6 / 4mm circular needles, configured for small circumference knitting, or size needed to obtain gauge

US#4 / 3.5mm circular needles, configured for small circumference knitting

Stitch markers

Large-eyed sewing needle

Gauge
22 sts and 28 rounds = 4 inches / 10 cm in pattern stitch, on larger needles

Pattern
With smaller needles and MC, cast on 112 (120, 132) sts. Being careful not to twist, join to work in the rnd. Place marker at start of rnd.

Rnd 1: *K2, p2; repeat from * to end of rnd.

Repeat Rnd 1 for 20 rnds total.

Rnd 21: Purl.

Change to larger needles and knit 1 (1, 2) rnds.

Join CC and work 32 rnds of Selbu Star chart as indicated for size.

Break CC and knit 1 (1, 2) rnds with MC. To lengthen the hat before crown decreases, work more rnds here.

Set up decrease rnds:

Remove marker, knit 14 (15, 16) sts, place marker. This is now the new start of the rnd.

Decrease as follows:

Rnd 1: *K13 (14, 15), s2kp, k12 (13, 14); repeat from * to end of rnd.

Rnds 2, 4, 6, 8, 10, 12: Knit.

Rnd 3: *K12 (13, 14), s2kp, k11 (12, 13); repeat from * to end of rnd.

Rnd 5: *K11 (12, 13), s2kp, k10 (11, 12); repeat from * to end of rnd.

Rnd 7: *K10 (11, 12), s2kp, k9 (10, 11); repeat from * to end of rnd.

Rnd 9: *K9 (10, 11), s2kp, k8 (9, 10); repeat from * to end of rnd.

Rnd 11: *K8 (9, 10), s2kp, k7 (8, 9); repeat from * to end of rnd.

Rnd 13: *K7 (8, 9), s2kp, k6 (7, 8); repeat from * to end of rnd.

Rnd 14: *K6 (7, 8), s2kp, k5 (6, 7); repeat from * to end of rnd.

Rnd 15: *K5 (6, 7), s2kp, k4 (5, 6); repeat from * to end of rnd.

Rnd 16: *K4 (5, 6), s2kp, k3 (4, 5); repeat from * to end of rnd.

Rnd 17: *K3 (4, 5), s2kp, k2 (3, 4)] repeat from * to end of rnd.

Rnd 18: *K2 (3, 4), s2kp, k1 (2, 3); repeat from * to end of rnd.

Rnd 19: *K1 (2, 3), s2kp, k0 (1, 2); repeat from * to end of rnd.

L (1X) sizes only:

Rnd 20: *K1 (2), s2kp, k0 (1); repeat from * to end of rnd.

1X size only:

Rnd 21: *K1, s2kp; repeat from * to end of rnd.

Break yarn, leaving a 12 inch / 30.5 cm end. Thread yarn needle. Work yarn needle through remaining sts. Pull taut to close top of hat and weave in ends.

Finishing

Fold ribbing into the inside of the hat, using purl ridge as a guide. Loosely tack ribbing to inside of hat. Block.

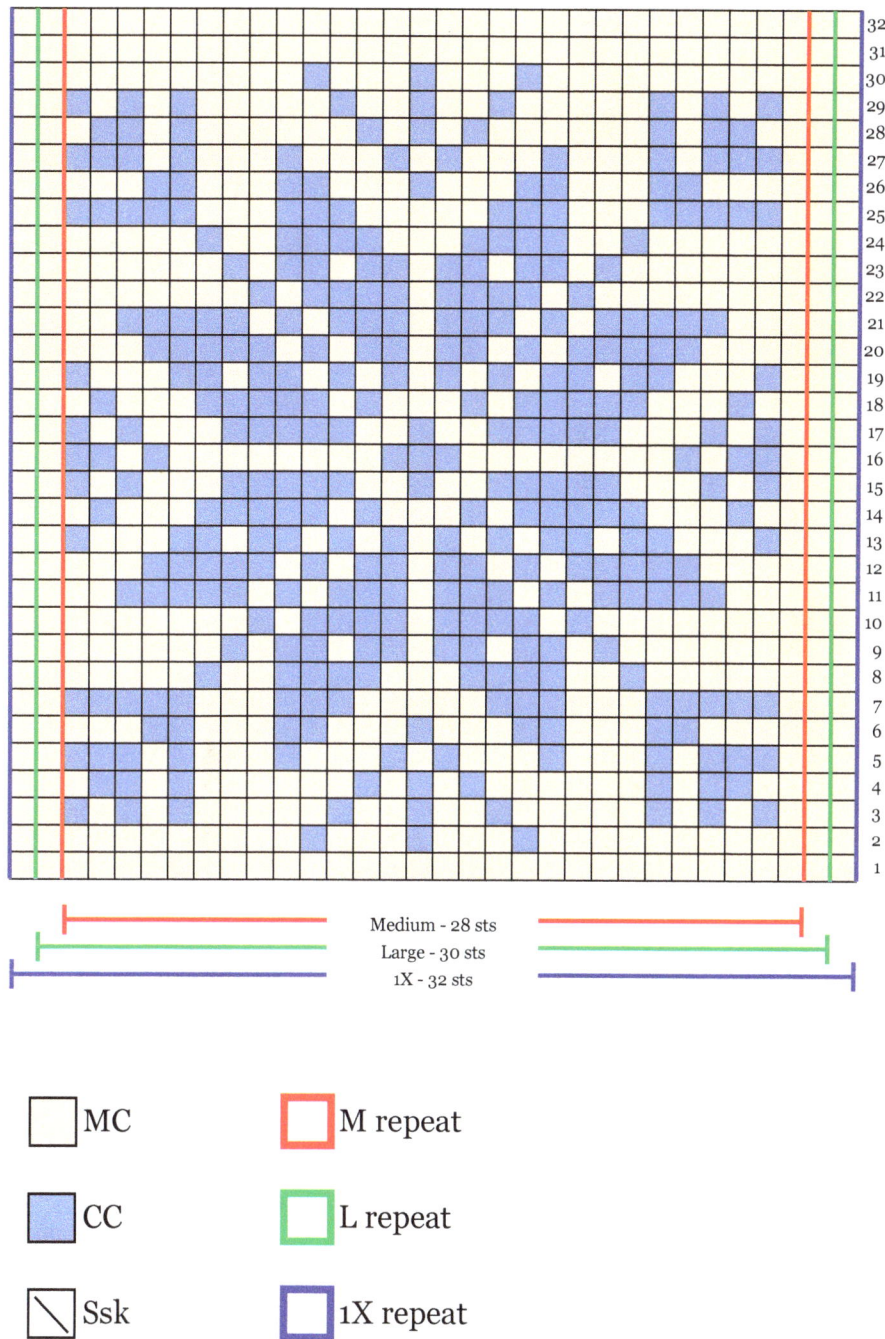

Medium - 28 sts
Large - 30 sts
1X - 32 sts

	MC			M repeat
	CC			L repeat
	Ssk			1X repeat

Wind and Stars

The color work pattern is a mosaic design with a modification of the repeat for the border. A contrasting hand-painted yarn or a gradient would also work well in this design. The top is shaped with an ssk (left-leaning decrease) at the end of each pattern repeat every third round.

Sizes
S (M, L, 1X)

Finished Measurements
Circumference 17.5 (20.25, 21.75, 23.25) inches / 44.5 (51.5, 55.75, 59) cm

Height to crown 5.5 (6.5, 7.5, 7.5) inches / 13.9 (16.5, 19, 19) cm

Materials
Blackberry Ridge Woolen Mill Sport Weight Natural Colored Wool (100% wool; 350 yds per 4 oz skein); MC color: Cream; 1 skein

Blackberry Ridge Woolen Mill Traditional Colors Sport Weight (100% wool; 350 yds per 4 oz skein); CC color: Charcoal; 1 skein

US#6 / 4mm circular needles, configured for small circumference knitting, or size needed to obtain gauge

US#4 / 3.5mm circular needles, configured for small circumference knitting

Stitch markers

Large-eyed sewing needle

Gauge
22 sts and 28 rounds = 4 inches / 10 cm in pattern stitch, on larger needles

Pattern
With smaller needles and MC, cast on 96 (112, 120, 128) sts. Leave a 12 inch / 30.5 cm tail for sewing up later.

Rows 1 - 9: Knit.

Change to larger needles.

Row 10: Knit.

Join to work in the round, placing a marker at start of rnd.

Rnd 11: Knit.

Join CC and work 30 (36, 43, 43) rnds of Wind and Stars main chart as indicated.

To lengthen or shorten your hat before the crown decreases, work more or less rnds of the main chart.

Please note that ending after a partial chart repeat will mean that the crown chart will not line up. If you're comfortable with the pattern however, it is quite easy to continue in pattern as set, working the decreases in the places set in the crown chart.

Work 19 rnds of Wind and Stars crown chart, working ssk decreases at the end of each repeat in the color indicated on chart.

Break yarn, leaving a 12 inch / 30.5 cm end.

Thread yarn needle. Work yarn needle through remaining sts. Pull taut to close top of hat and weave in ends.

Finishing

Using cast on tail, neatly seam garter st band. Weave in ends.

Block.

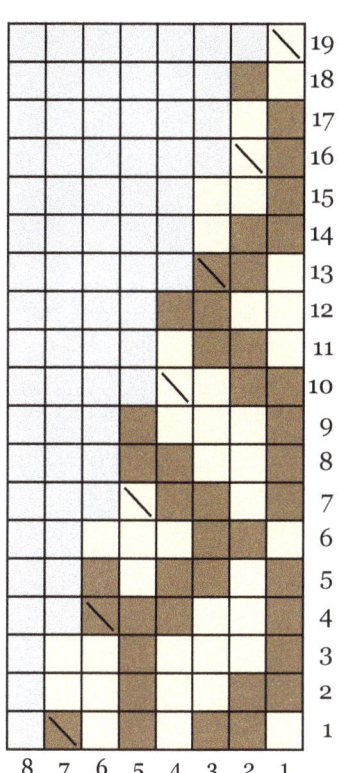

Crown Chart

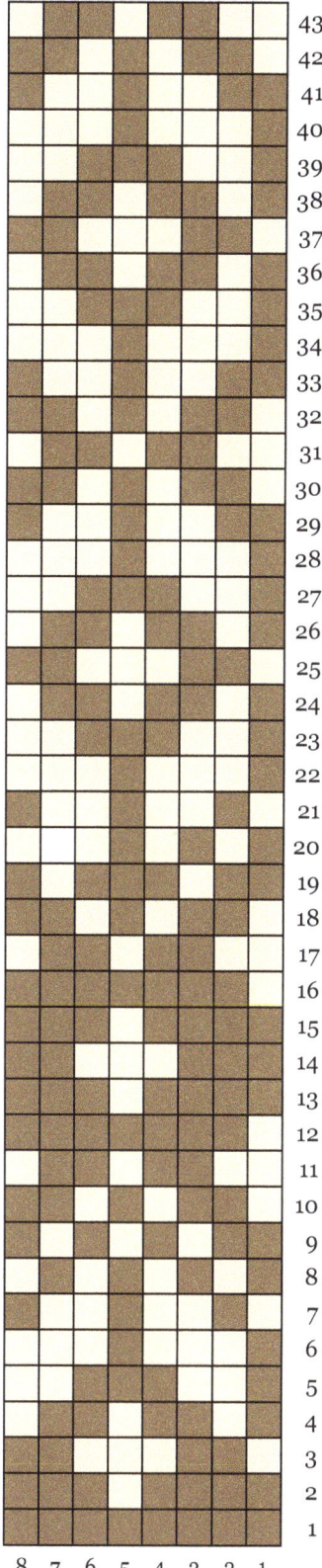

No stitch

MC

CC

Ssk

Main Chart

Selbu Star Redux

This hat has the Selbu Rose/Star as the top of the hat. It is formed by double decreases which shape the crown. While only written in one size, you could make it smaller by knitting at a tighter gauge (more stitches per inch/cm) or larger by knitting at a looser gauge (fewer stitches per inch/cm).

One size
Large

Finished Measurements
Circumference 22 inches / 55.75 cm

Height to crown 7.5 inches / 19 cm

Total height 10.25 inches / 26 cm

Materials
Blackberry Ridge Woolen Mill Sport Weight Natural Colored Wool (100% wool; 350 yds per 4 oz skein); MC color: Cream; 1 skein

Blackberry Ridge Woolen Mill Traditional Colors Sport Weight (100% wool; 350 yds per 4 oz skein); CC color: Charcoal; 1 skein

US#6 / 4mm circular needles, configured for small circumference knitting, or size needed to obtain gauge

US#4 / 3.5mm circular needles, configured for small circumference knitting

Stitch markers

Large-eyed sewing needle

Gauge
22 sts and 28 rounds = 4 inches / 10 cm in pattern stitch, on larger needles

Pattern
With smaller needles and MC, cast on 120 sts. Leave a 12 inch / 30.5 cm tail for sewing up later.

Rows 1 - 9: Knit.

Switch to larger needles.

Row 10: Knit.

Being careful not to twist, join to work in the rnd. Place marker at start of rnd.

Rnd 11: Knit.

Join CC and follow Selbu Star Redux main chart as indicated, repeating Rnds 18-25, 3 times, until Rnd 28 is completed.

Shorten length by ending on Rnd 25 and then decreasing top following chart on Rnd 26 to end. To lengthen, repeat Rnds 18-25 until desired length and the decrease top by following Rnd 26 to end.

Rnd 29: Work S2kp decrease in color as indicated in chart. Begin each round with s2kp by:

- working to 1 st before the marker,
- slip this st to the right hand needle,
- remove marker,
- place slipped st back onto left hand needle,
- replace marker,
- work the s2kp in CC and continue across chart.

Continue until Rnd 43 has been completed.

Break yarn, leaving a 12 inch / 30.5 cm end. Thread yarn needle. Work yarn needle through remaining sts. Pull taut to close top of hat and weave in ends.

Finishing
Using cast on tail, neatly seam garter st band. Weave in ends.

Block.

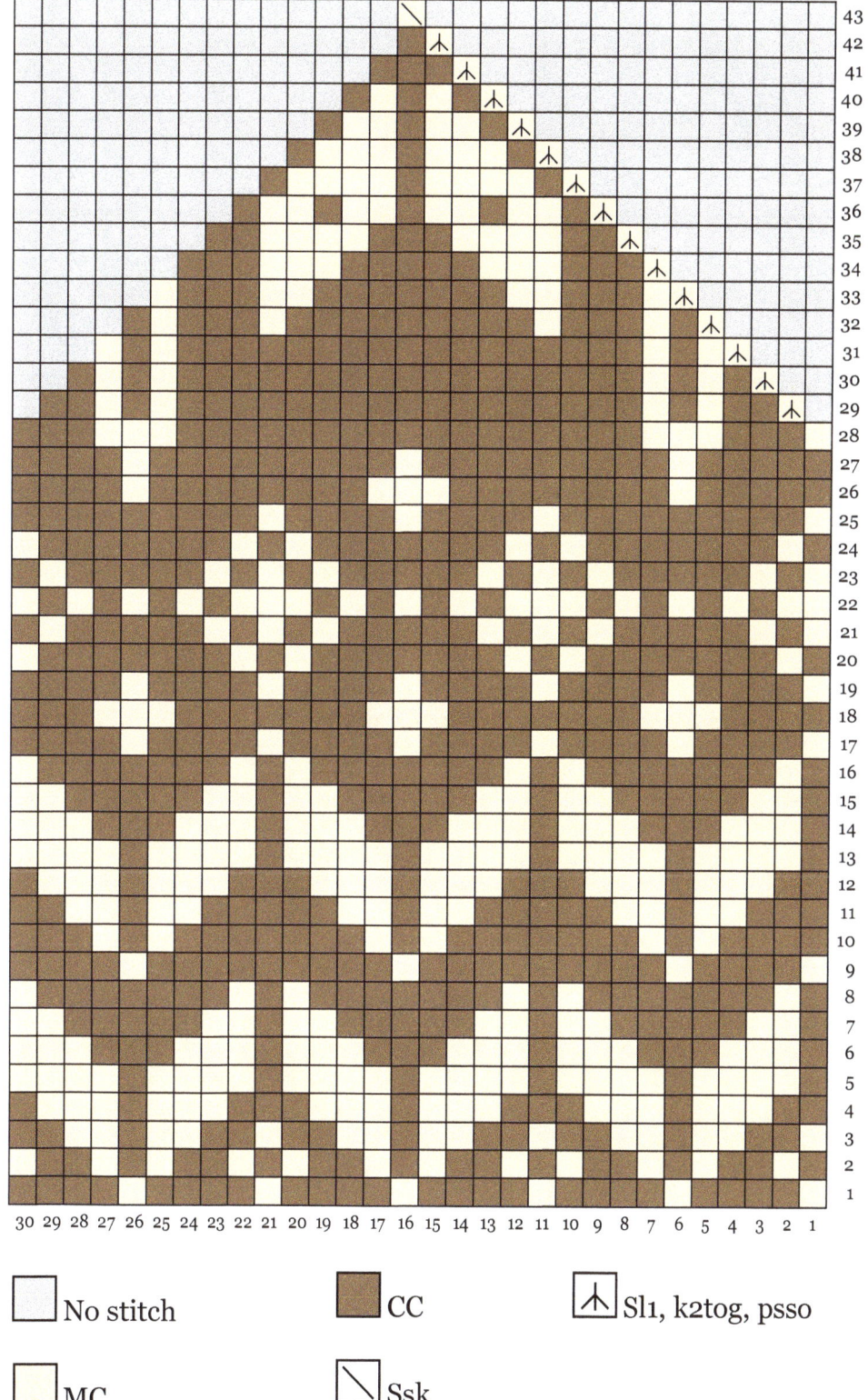

	No stitch		CC		Sl1, k2tog, psso
	MC		Ssk		

Trøndelag at Night

Reversing light and dark in this version of the Trondelag hat resulted in a darker crown. A garter stitch band and fewer rounds make this hat a quicker knit.

Sizes
S (M, L, 1X)

Finished Measurements
Circumference 17.5 (19.75, 21.75, 23.25) inches /44.5 (49.5, 55.25, 59) cm

Height to crown 7.25 (9, 9, 9) inches / 18 (22.75, 22.75, 22.75) cm

Total height 10.25 (12.25, 12.25, 12.25) inches / 26 (31.25, 31.25, 31.25) cm

Materials
Blackberry Ridge Woolen Mill Sport Weight Natural Colored Wool (100% wool; 350 yds per 4 oz skein); MC color: Cream; 1 skein

Blackberry Ridge Woolen Mill Sport Weight Kaleidoscope Yarn (100% wool; 180 yds per 2 oz skein); CC color: Joyce's Choice; 1 skein

US#6 / 4 mm circular needles, configured for circular knitting, or size needed to obtain gauge

US#4 / 3.5 mm circular needles, configured for circular knitting

Stitch markers

Large-eyed sewing needle

Gauge
22 sts and 28 rounds = 4 inches / 10 cm in pattern stitch, on larger needles

Pattern
With smaller needles and MC, cast on 96 (108, 120, 132) sts. Leave a 12 inch / 30.5 cm tail for sewing up later.

Rnds 1 - 9: Knit.

Change to larger needles.

Rnd 10: Knit.

Being careful not to twist, join to work in the rnd. Place marker at start of rnd.

Rnd 11: Knit.

Join CC, and work 1 (2, 2, 2) full repeats of Rnds 1 - 14 of Trøndelag at Night chart. Repeat Rnds 1 - 7. (Toddler Size: 21 rnds total. All Other Sizes: 35 rnds total).

If you would like to change the height of your hat, work further rnds of Trøndelag at Night chart. Please note that ending after a partial chart repeat will mean that the crown chart will not line up. If you're comfortable with the pattern however, it is quite easy to continue in pattern as set, working the decreases in the places set in the crown chart.

When completed, begin following Trøndelag at Night Decrease Chart. Work ssk decreases at the end of each repeat in color indicated on chart.

Break yarn, leaving a 12 inch / 30.5 cm end. Thread yarn needle. Work yarn needle through remaining sts. Pull taut to close top of hat and weave in ends.

Finishing
Using cast on tail, neatly seam garter st band. Weave in ends.

Block.

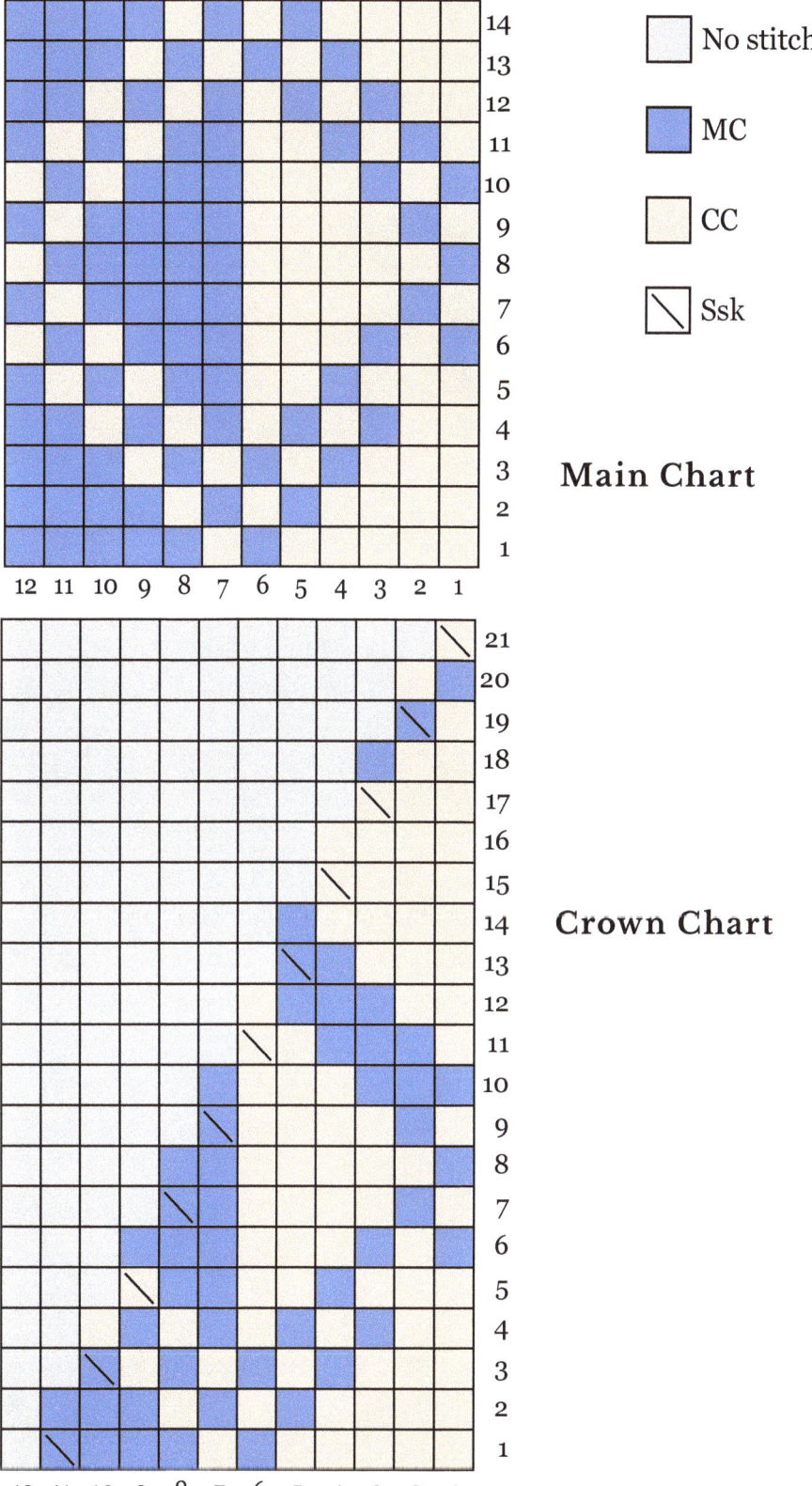

Main Chart

Crown Chart

No stitch

MC

CC

Ssk

Rose Mandala

A simple Norwegian motif is paired with a lice stitch to shorten the floats. The colors are reversed for one repeat and then reversed again. To shape the crown, an ssk (left-leaning decrease) is worked at the end of each pattern repeat with a surprising result. Substituting a gradient dyed yarn or a speckle for the hand-painted yarn would be lovely.

Sizes
S (M, L, 1X)

Finished Measurements
Circumference 17.5 (20.25, 21.75, 24.75) inches / 44.5 (51.5, 55.25, 62.75) cm

Height to crown 5.75 (7.75, 7.75, 7.75) inches / 14.5 (19.75, 19.75, 19.75) cm

Total height 8.5 (10.25, 10.25, 10.25) inches / 21.5 (26, 26, 26) cm

Materials
Blackberry Ridge Woolen Mill Traditional Colors Sport Weight (100% wool; 350 yds per 4 oz skein); MC color: Black; 1 skein

Blackberry Ridge Woolen Mill Sport Weight Kaleidoscope Yarn (100% wool; 180 yds per 2 oz skein); CC color: Tropical Fish; 1 skein

US#6 / 4 mm circular needles, configured for circular knitting, or size needed to obtain gauge

US#4 / 3.5 mm circular needles, configured for circular knitting

Stitch markers

Large-eyed sewing needle

Gauge
22 sts and 28 rounds = 4 inches / 10 cm in pattern stitch, on larger needles

Pattern
With smaller needles and MC, cast on 96 (112, 120, 136) sts, leaving a 12 inch / 30.5 cm tail for joining later.

Rows 1 - 9: Knit.

Change to larger needles.

Row 10: Knit.

Being careful not to twist, join to work in the round. Place marker at start of round.

Small size only: Work Rnds 1 - 30 of Rose Mandala chart, then Rnds 44 - 62.

All other sizes: Work Rnds 1 - 62 of Rose Mandala chart

To adjust height, work to the desired length before the crown shaping, then continue in pattern as set, using ssk decreases at the end of every third rnd of pattern repeat.

Break yarn, leaving a 12 inch / 30.5 cm end. Thread yarn needle. Work yarn needle through remaining sts. Pull taut to close top of hat and weave in ends.

Finishing
Neatly seam garter st band. Weave in ends.

Block.

☐ No stitch   ☐ CC

■ MC   ◻ Ssk

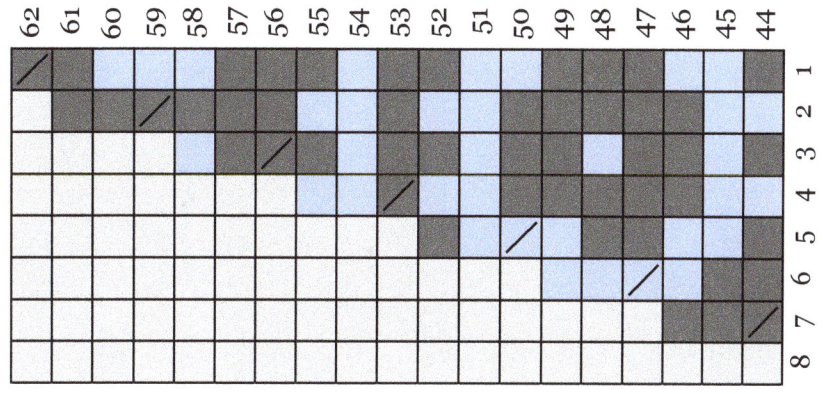

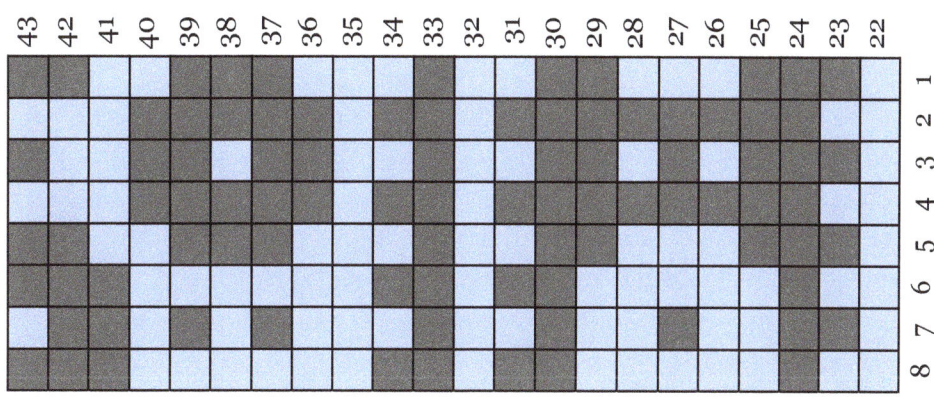

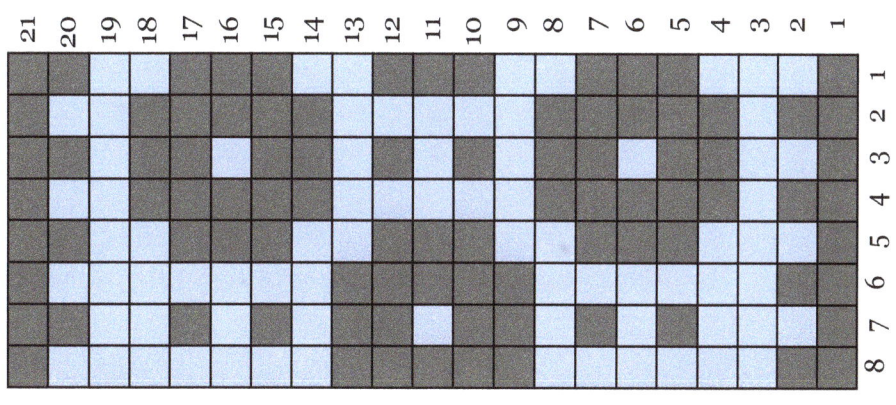

Chorus Girl

Reminiscent of chorus girls' rehearsal costumes in 1940's musicals, this hat is a simple and quick knit. Narrow stripes on the garter stitch band contrast with the wide stripes on the body of the hat. At the crown, the stripes are abandoned and a decrease is done at six points every other round. The color pooling effect will vary depending on the hat size and yarn chosen.

Sizes
S (M, L, 1X)

Finished Measurements
Circumference 17.5 (20.25, 21.75, 24.75) inches / 44.5 (51.5, 55.25, 62.75) cm

Height to crown 7.25 (9.25, 9.25, 9.25) inches / 18.5 (23.5, 23.5, 23.5) cm

Total height 9.75 (11.75, 11.75, 11.75) inches / 24.75 (30, 30, 30) cm

Materials
Blackberry Ridge Woolen Mill Sport Weight Natural Colored Wool (100% wool; 350 yds per 4 oz skein); MC color: Cream; 1 skein

Blackberry Ridge Woolen Mill Sport Weight Kaleidoscope Yarn (100% wool; 180 yds per 2 oz skein); CC color: Tropical Fish; 1 skein

US#6 / 4 mm circular needles, configured for circular knitting, or size needed to obtain gauge

US#4 / 3.5 mm circular needles, configured for circular knitting

Stitch markers

Large-eyed sewing needle

Gauge
22 sts and 28 rounds = 4 inches / 10 cm in pattern stitch, on larger needles

Pattern Note
Your pooling will vary depending on hat size and yarn chosen.

Pattern
With smaller needles and MC, cast on 96 (108, 120, 132) sts, leaving a 12 inch / 30.5 cm tail for sewing up later.

Working back forth, knit as follows:

Rows 1 and 2: With MC, knit.

Rows 3 and 4: With CC, knit.

Rows 5 and 6: With MC, knit.

Rows 7 and 8: With CC, knit.

Rows 9 and 10: With MC, knit.

Rows 11 and 12: With CC, knit.

Rows 13 and 14: With MC, knit.

Change to larger needles.

Row 15: With MC, knit.

Join to work in the round.

Rnds 16 and 17: With MC, knit.

Rnds 18 - 27: With CC, knit.

Rnds 28 and 29: With MC, knit.

Rnds 30 - 39: With CC, knit.

Rnds 40 and 41: With MC, knit.

Rnds 42 - 51: With CC, knit.

Sizes M, L, and 1X only:

Rnds 52 and 53: With MC, knit.

Rnds 54 - 63: With CC, knit.

All sizes:

Break CC.

Rnds 64 and 65: With MC, knit.

To adjust height, work to desired length to crown. Work 2 rnds with MC and begin decreasing top of hat as described.

Begin decreasing top of hat as follows:

Rnd 1: *K10, k2tog; repeat from * to end of rnd.

Rnd 2: Knit.

Rnd 3: *K9, k2tog; repeat from * to end of rnd.

Rnd 4: Knit.

Rnd 5: *K8, k2tog; repeat from * to end of rnd.

Rnd 6: Knit.

Rnd 7: *K7, k2tog; repeat from * to end of rnd.

Rnd 8: Knit.

Rnd 9: *K6, k2tog; repeat from * to end of rnd.

Rnd 10: Knit.

Rnd 11: *K5, k2tog; repeat from * to end of rnd.

Rnd 12: Knit.

Rnd 13: *K4, k2tog; repeat from * to end of rnd.

Rnd 14: *K3, k2tog; repeat from * to end of rnd.

Rnd 15: *K2, k2tog; repeat from * to end of rnd.

Rnd 16: *K1, k2tog; repeat from * to end of rnd.

Rnd 17: *K2tog; repeat from * to end of rnd.

Break yarn, leaving a 12 inch / 30.5 cm end. Thread yarn needle. Work yarn needle through remaining sts. Pull taut to close top of hat. Weave in ends.

Finishing
Neatly seam garter st band. Weave in ends.

Block.

Prim Check and Ribbon

A houndstooth check hat that can be dressed up or down. The knitting begins with an easy and fun Latvian twisted garter stitch cast on. The "ribbon" is simple garter stitch stripes. Finish by sewing on a knitted bow and smocking the "ribbon" every third pattern repeat.

Sizes

S (M, L, 1X)

Circumference 17.5 (20.25, 21.75, 24.75) inches / 44.5 (51.5, 55.25, 62.75) cm

Height to crown 5.75 (7.5, 7.5, 7.5) inches / 14.5 (19, 19, 19) cm

Total height 8.75 (10.5, 10.5, 10.5) inches / 22.25 (26.75, 26.75, 26.75) cm

Materials

Blackberry Ridge Woolen Mill Sport Weight Natural Colored Wool (100% wool; 350 yds per 4 oz skein); MC color: Cream; 1 skein

Blackberry Ridge Woolen Mill Sport Weight Kaleidoscope Yarn (100% wool; 180 yds per 2 oz skein); CC color: Black; 1 skein

US#6 / 4 mm circular needles, configured for circular knitting, or size needed to obtain gauge

US#4 / 3.5 mm circular needles, configured for circular knitting

Stitch markers

Large-eyed sewing needle

Gauge

22 sts and 28 rounds = 4 inches / 10 cm in pattern stitch, on larger needles

Pattern

With smaller needles and MC, cast on 96 (108, 120, 132) sts, leaving a 12 inch / 30.5 cm tail for joining later.

Rows 1 and 2: Knit.

Break MC.

Join CC.

Row 3: Work Twisted Garter st as follows: *K6, rotate RH needle 360 degrees clockwise, bring yarn between the two needles and then to the back of your work; repeat from * to end of row.

Attach MC.

Rows 4 and 5: With MC, knit.

Rows 6 and 7: With CC, knit.

Rows 8 - 13: With MC, knit.

Rows 14 and 15: With CC, knit.

Change to larger needles.

Row 16: With MC, knit.

Join to work in the round, placing a marker at start of round.

Work Prim Check and Ribbon main chart 6 (9, 9, 9) times, a total of 24 (36, 36, 36) rnds, or to desired length, ending after Rnd 4 of the chart repeat.

Follow Prim Check and Ribbon Hat decrease chart for top of hat. Work ssk decreases in color as indicated on chart.

Break yarn, leaving a 12 inch / 30.5 cm end. Thread yarn needle. Work yarn needle through remaining sts. Pull taut to close top of hat. Weave in ends.

Bow:

With CC, and larger needle, cast on 30 sts. K 2 rows.

Rows 1 and 2: Knit.

Attach MC

Rows 3 - 8: With MC, knit.

Rows 9 and 10: With CC, knit.

Seam short edges together. Center seam to the back. With MC yarn, wrap tightly around the middle of bow to draw it together. Secure on the back and leave end for sewing to hat.

Finishing

Seam garter st band. Weave in ends. With MC, wrap every third pattern on garter st ribbon. Skim yarn loosely across inside of hat between wraps.

Sew on bow.

Block.

 No stitch

 MC

 CC

 Ssk

Main Chart

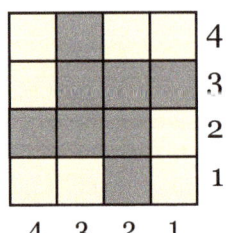

Crown Chart

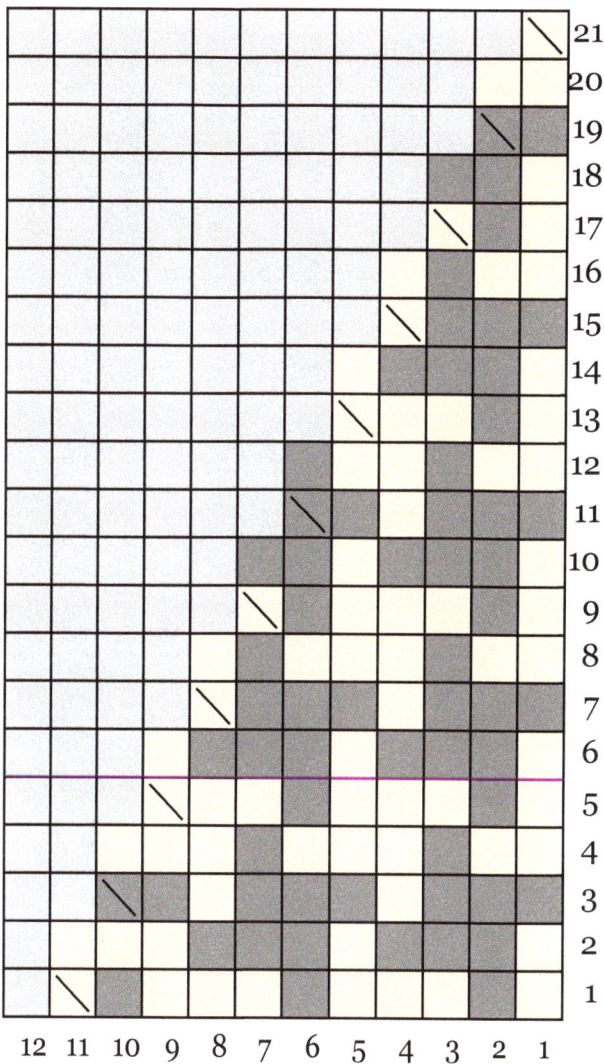

Miter Box

This hat is knitted flat with a series of mitered squares and garter stitch ridges. The length can be easily adjusted by knitting more or fewer garter stitch rows. A stretchy bind off is used for the garter stitch band. Modular knitting is a color playground! Try knitting each mitered square a different color. Or try knitting the mitered squares one color and the garter stitch ridges a different color. Gradient dyed and speckled yarn can be used to great effect as well. Make it your own!

Sizes
S (M, L, 1X)

Finished Measurements
Circumference 17.75 (19.75, 21.75, 23.75) inches / 45 (50, 55.25, 60.25) cm

Height to crown 5 (6.25, 6.75, 9.25) inches / 12.5 (16, 17.5, 21) cm

Total height 7 (8.5, 9.25, 11) inches / 18 (21.5, 23.5, 28) cm

Materials
Blackberry Ridge Woolen Mill Worsted Kaleidoscope Yarn (100% Wool; 230 yds per 4 oz skein); Color: Firecracker; 1 skein

US#8 / 5mm straight needles, or size needed to obtain gauge

Large-eyed sewing needle

Gauge
16 sts and 32 rows = 4 inches / 10 cm in garter stitch

Pattern
Cast on 19 (21, 23, 25) sts.

Knitting back forth, work as follows:

Row 1: Knit. Turn.

Row 2: K8 (9, 10, 11), k3tog, k8 (9, 10, 11). Turn.

Row 3 (and all odd rows): Knit.

Row 4: K7 (8, 9, 10), k3tog, k7 (8, 9, 10). Turn.

Row 6: K6 (7, 8, 9), k3tog, k6 (7, 8, 9). Turn.

Row 8: K5 (6, 7, 8), k3tog, k 5 (6, 7, 8). Turn.

Row 10: K4 (5, 6, 7), k3tog, k4 (5, 6, 7). Turn.

Row 12: K3 (4, 5, 6), k3tog, k 3 (4, 5, 6). Turn.

Row 14: K2 (3, 4, 5), k3tog, k2 (3, 4, 5). Turn.

Row 16: K1 (2, 3, 4), k3tog, k1 (2, 3, 4). Turn.

Row 18: K0 (1, 2, 3), k3tog, k0 (1, 2, 3). Turn.

Row 19: K1, (3, 5, 7) sts.

Sizes M (L, 1X) only

Row 20: K 0 (1, 2), k3tog, k0 (1, 2). Turn.

Size L (1X) only

Row 22: K0 (1), k3tog, k0 (1). Turn.

Size 1X only

Row 24: K3tog. Turn.

Row 25: Knit 1.

All sizes:

Pick up and knit 8 (9, 10, 12) sts along the left side of the square as it faces you.

Cast on 10 (11, 12, 13) sts. Turn. 17, (19, 21, 23) sts.

Repeat Rows 1 - 19 (21, 23, 25).

Continue in this manner, knitting a mitered square and then picking up and casting on sts to knit the next mitered square until 8 mitered squares are completed.

Turn work. Pick up and knit 71 (79, 87, 95) sts along the top of the row of mitered squares. 72 (80, 88, 96) sts.

Knit 3 (5, 5, 5) rows. To adjust height to crown knit more or fewer odd number of rows here.

Cast on 10 (11, 12, 13) sts. Turn.

Knit across 19 (21, 23, 25) sts. Turn.

Repeat Rows 2 - 19 (21, 23, 25) to complete the first mitered square of the row.

Pick up and knit 8 (9, 10, 11) sts down the left side of the square as it faces you and then knit the next 10 (11, 12, 13) sts of the waiting sts on the needle. Turn.

Repeat Rows 2 - 23 to complete the next mitered square. Continue in this manner, knitting a mitered square and then picking up and knitting across waiting sts to knit the next mitered square until 8 mitered squares are completed.

Turn work. Pick up and knit 71 (79, 87, 95) sts along the top of the row of mitered squares. 72 (80, 88, 96) sts.

Knit 3 (5, 5, 5) rows. To adjust height to crown knit more or fewer odd number of rows here.

Begin decreasing top of hat:

Row 1: *K7 (8, 9, 10), k2tog; repeat from * to end of row.

Row 2 (and all even rows): Knit.

Row 3: *K6 (7, 8, 9), k2tog; repeat from * to end of row.

Row 5: *K5 (6, 7, 8), k2tog; repeat from * to end of row.

Row 7: *K4, (5, 6, 7), k2tog; repeat from * to end of row.

Row 9: *K3, (4, 5, 6), k2tog; repeat from * to end of row.

Row 11: *K2, (3, 4, 5), k2tog; repeat from * to end of row.

Row 13: *K1, (2, 3, 4), k2tog; repeat from * to end of row.

Row 15: *K0 (1, 2, 3) , k2tog; repeat from * to end of row.

Sizes M (L, 1X) only

Row 17: *K0 (1, 2), k2tog; repeat from * to end of row.

Sizes L (1X) only

Row 19: *K0 (1), k2tog; repeat from * to end of row.

Size 1X only

Row 17:*K2tog; repeat from * to end of row.

Break yarn, leaving a 12 inch / 30.5 cm end. Thread yarn needle. Work yarn needle through remaining sts. Leave end for later to close top hat and to seam side.

Pick up and knit 72 (80, 88, 96) sts at bottom of hat.

Knit 3 (5, 5, 3) rows. Bind off loosely or use this variation of a Jeny's Surprisingly Stretchy Bind Off:

http://bit.ly/jenysss

K1, * wrap yarn around needle the opposite way than usual, k1, pass first k1 and yo over second k1 st; repeat from * to end of row.

Pull yarn through last st. Break yarn and leave a 12 inch / 30.5 cm end for sewing up and weaving in.

Finishing

Pull waiting end taut to close top of hat.

Neatly seam garter ridges together and weave in ends.

Block.

Pythagorean Band Beret

This hat boasts a modular knit band of nesting triangles. Stitches are doubled in number and then are quickly decreased as the hat is worked flat in garter stitch. Have fun playing with color in the band. Perhaps add stripes to the body of the hat?

Sizes
S (M, L, 1X)

Finished Measurements
Circumference 17.75 (19.75, 21.75, 23.75) inches / 45 (50, 55.25, 60.25) cm

Total height 7.25 (8.25, 9, 12.25) inches / 19.5 (21, 23, 31) cm

Materials
Blackberry Ridge Woolen Mill Medium Weight/Worsted Weight Traditional Colors (100% wool; 230 yds per 4 oz skein); MC: Colonial Blue; 1 skein CC1: Aster, 1 skein. CC2: Light Blue, 1 skein.

US#8 / 5 mm straight needles, or size needed to obtain gauge.

US H / 5mm crochet hook

Stitch markers

Large-eyed sewing needle

Gauge
16 sts and 32 rows = 4 inches / 10 cm in garter st

Pattern
Section 1

With CC 1, cast on 56 (64, 72, 80) sts, leaving a 12 inch / 30.5 cm tail for sewing up later.

Knitting back forth, knit half-triangles as follows:

[K1, turn, k1 turn

K2, turn, k2 turn

K3, turn, k3 turn

K4, turn, k4 turn

K5, turn, k5 turn

K6, turn, k6 turn

K7, turn, k7 turn

K8, turn, k8, do not turn.]

Repeat 6 (7, 8, 9) times. Turn. Break CC1. 7 (8, 9, 10) half-triangles.

Section 2

With CC2, cast 8 sts onto needle with waiting sts.

[K7, ssk, (ssk will be one CC2 st and one CC1 st), turn, k6, k2tog. Turn.

K6, ssk, turn, k5, k2tog. Turn.

K5, ssk, turn, k4, k2tog. Turn.

K4, ssk, turn, k3, k2tog. Turn.

K3, ssk, turn, k2, k2tog. Turn.

K2, ssk, turn, k1, k2tog. Turn.

K1, ssk, turn, k2tog. Turn.

Ssk. Do not turn.

Pick up and knit 7 sts on side of half-triangle. Turn.

K8, turn]

Repeat 6 (7, 8, 9) times. Break yarn. Fasten off.

Section 3

With MC, pick up and knit 56 (64, 72, 80) sts along top of CC 2 line of triangles.

Next row: Kfb in each st across row. 112 (128, 144, 160) sts.

Knit 5 rows.

Next row: Decrease 2 (8, 4, 0) sts evenly spaced across row. 110 (120, 140, 160) sts

Knit 1 row.

Size 1X only

Decrease Row: *K14, k2tog; repeat from * to end of row. (150) sts

Knit 7 rows.

Decrease Row: *K13, k2tog; repeat from * to end of row. (140) sts

Knit 7 rows.

Sizes L (1X) only

Decrease Row: *K12, k2tog; repeat from * to end of row. (130) sts

Knit 7 rows.

Decrease Row: *K11, k2tog; repeat from * to end of row. (120) sts

Knit 7 rows.

Sizes M (L, 1X) only

Decrease Row: *K10, k2tog; repeat from * to end of row. (110) sts

Knit 7 rows.

All sizes

Decrease Row: *K9, k2tog; repeat from * to end of row. (100) sts

Knit 7 rows.

Decrease Row: *K8, k2tog; repeat from * to end of row. (90) sts

Knit 7 rows.

Decrease Row: *K7, k2tog; repeat from * to end of row. (80) sts

Knit 7 rows.

Decrease Row: *K6, k2tog; repeat from * to end of row. (70) sts

Knit 1 row.

Decrease Row: *K5, k2tog; repeat from * to end of row. (60) sts

Knit 1 row.

Decrease Row: *K4, k2tog; repeat from * to end of row. (50) sts

Knit 1 row.

Decrease Row: *K3, k2tog] repeat to end of row. (40) sts

K 1 row.

Decrease Row: *K2, k2tog; repeat from * to end of row. (30) sts

Knit 1 row.

Decrease Row: *K1, k2tog; repeat from * to end of row. (20) sts

Knit 1 row.

Decrease Row: *K2tog; repeat from * to end of row. (10) sts

Decrease Row: *K2tog; repeat from * to end of row. (5) sts

Break yarn, leaving a 12 inch / 30.5 cm end. Thread yarn needle. Work yarn needle through remaining sts. Pull taut to close top of hat.

Finishing

Neatly seam garter st band together. Weave in ends.

With MC, and crochet hook, work 1 round of single crochet around bottom of hat.

Block.

Do-Si-Do

This hat is a simple 1x1 ribbing pattern with a cable cross on every fifth round. The crown has a fun shaping as the cable cross continues as the work decreases. It is easy to knit with just enough going on to make it interesting. Try knitting it with a worsted weight gradient dyed or a speckled yarn for a different look.

Sizes
S (M, L, 1X)

Finished Measurements
Circumference 17.75 (19.5, 21.5, 23) inches / 45 (49.5, 54.5, 58.5) cm

Height to crown 6.5 (7.25, 8, 8.75) inches / 16.5 (18.5, 20, 22.25) cm

Total height 8 (9, 9.75, 10.5) inches / 20 (23, 24.75, 26.75) cm

Materials
Blackberry Ridge Woolen Mill Medium Weight/Worsted Weight Traditional Colors (100% Wool; 230 yds per 4 oz skein); Color: Colonial Blue; 1 skein (On model – Color: Burgundy)

US#8 / 5 mm needles, configured for circular knitting, or size needed to obtain gauge

Large-eyed sewing needle

Cable needle

Stitch marker

Gauge
18 sts and 25 rounds = 4 inches / 10 cm in pattern stitch

Pattern
Cast on 80 (88, 96, 104) sts. Being careful not to twist, join to work in the round. Place marker at the beginning of the rnd.

Rnds 1 - 4: *P1, k1; repeat from * to end of rnd.

Rnd 5: *P1, 1 / 2 RC; repeat from * to end of rnd.

Repeat these 5 rnds, 8 (9, 10, 11) times.

To adjust the height, work to desired length, ending after Rnd 5 of pattern, then work top decrease, as below.

Decrease top

Rnd 1: *K2tog, p1, k1; repeat from * to end of rnd. 60 (66, 72, 78) sts.

Rnds 2 and 3: *K1, p1, k1; repeat

from * to end of rnd.

Rnd 4: *1 / 2 RC repeat from * to end of rnd.

Rnd 5: *K2tog, p1; repeat from * to end of rnd. 40 (44, 48, 52) sts.

Rnds 6-8: *K1, p1; repeat from * to end of rnd.

Rnd 9: *K2tog; repeat from * to end of rnd. 20 (22, 24, 26) sts.

Rnd 10: Knit.

Rnd 11: *K2tog; repeat from * to end of rnd. 10 (11, 12, 13) sts.

Finishing

Break yarn, leaving a 12 inch / 30.5 cm end. Thread yarn needle. Work yarn needle through remaining sts. Pull taut to close top of hat. Weave in ends.

Block.

Big Top Stocking Cap

Do stocking hats ever go out of style? They are so much fun to knit and wear. Using a selfstriping yarn makes the work easy. Try designing your own stripes or stranded color work pattern with yarn from your stash.

Sizes
S (M, L, 1X)

Finished Measurements
Circumference 17 (19, 21.5, 24) inches / 43.25 (48.25, 54.5, 61) cm

Height to crown 6 inches / 15.25 cm

Total height 17.75 (23.75, 25.5, 27.5) inches / 45 (60.5, 64.75, 70) inches

Materials
Universal Yarn Classic Worsted Tapestry (80% Acrylic / 20% Wool; 197 yds per 100g skein); Color: Sweetheart; 2 skeins

US#4 / 3.5 mm needles, configured for circular knitting, or two sizes smaller than size needed to obtain gauge

US#6 / 4 mm needles, configured for circular knitting, or size needed to obtain gauge

Large-eyed sewing needle

Stitch marker

Gauge
18 sts and 24 rounds = 4 inches / 10 cm in stockinette stitch

Pattern
With smaller needles, cast on 84 (90, 98, 108) sts. Being careful not to twist, join to work in the round. Place marker at the beginning of the rnd.

Rnds 1 - 10: *K1, p1; repeat from * to end of rnd.

Change to larger needles and increase 0 (6, 10, 12) sts evenly spaced on first rnd.

Knit 24 rnds, or length desired.

Decrease top

1X size only

Decrease Rnd: *K18, k2tog; repeat from * to end of rnd. (114 sts).

Knit 5 rnds.

Sizes L (1X) only

Decrease Rnd: *K17, k2tog; repeat from * to end of rnd. (108 sts).

Knit 5 rnds.

Sizes M (L, 1X) only

Decrease Rnd: *K16, k2tog; repeat from * to end of rnd. (102 sts).

Knit 5 rnds.

All Sizes

Decrease Rnd 1: *K15, k2tog; repeat from * to end of rnd. (96 sts).

Knit 5 rnds.

Decrease Rnd 2: *K14, k2tog; repeat from * to end of rnd. (90 sts).

Knit 5 rnds.

Decrease Rnd 3: *K13, k2tog; repeat from * to end of rnd. (84 sts).

Knit 5 rnds.

Decrease Rnd 4: *K12, k2tog; repeat from * to end of rnd. (78 sts).

Knit 5 rnds.

Decrease Rnd 5: *K11, k2tog; repeat from * to end of rnd. (72 sts).

Knit 5 rnds.

Decrease Rnd 6: *K10, k2tog; repeat from * to end of rnd. (66 sts).

Knit 5 rnds.

Decrease Rnd 7: *K9, k2tog; repeat from * to end of rnd. (60 sts).

Knit 5 rnds.

Decrease Rnd 8: *K8, k2tog; repeat from * to end of rnd. (54 sts).

Knit 5 rnds.

Decrease Rnd 9: *K7, k2tog; repeat from * to end of rnd. (48 sts).

Knit 5 rnds.

Decrease Rnd 10: *K6, k2tog; repeat from * to end of rnd. (42 sts).

Knit 5 rnds.

Decrease Rnd 11: *K5, k2tog; repeat from * to end of rnd. (36 sts).

Knit 5 rnds.

Decrease Rnd 12: *K4, k2tog; repeat from * to end of rnd. (30 sts).

Knit 5 rnds.

Decrease Rnd 13: *K3, k2tog; repeat from * to end of rnd. (24 sts).

Knit 5 rnds.

Decrease Rnd 14: *K2, k2tog; repeat

from * to end of rnd. (18 sts).

Knit 5 rnds.

Decrease Rnd 15: *K1, k2tog; repeat from * to end of rnd. (12 sts).

Knit 5 rnds.

Decrease Rnd 16: *K2tog; repeat from * to end of rnd. (6 sts).

Finishing

Break yarn, leaving a 12 inch / 30.5 cm end. Thread yarn needle. Work yarn needle through remaining sts. Pull taut to close top of hat. Weave in ends.

Block.

Make a tassel and attach to top of hat.

See directions in introduction for making a tassel.

Slanted Columns

In this hat, the diagonal rib pattern offsets the striping of the yarn. Although it looks complicated, the stitch pattern is a simple six stitch repeat.

Sizes
S (M, L, 1X)

Finished Measurements
To fit 18 (20, 22, 24) inches / 45.75 (50.75, 55.75, 61) cm slightly stretched

Circumference 16.75 (19.25, 21.75, 24) inches / 45.5 (49, 55.25, 61) cm

Height to crown 7 (9, 9, 9) inches / 17.75 (22.75, 22.75, 22.75) cm

Total height 9.25 (11.25, 11.25, 11.25) inches / 23.5 (28.5, 28.5, 28.5) cm

Materials
Adriafil KNITCOL ART.KN (100% Merino Super wash; 137 yds per 50g skein); Color: Giotto Fancy; 2 skeins

On model: Lang Yarns Jawoll Magic 6Ply (75% Wool / 25% Nylon; 459 yds per 150g skein); Color: 18; 1 skein

US#4 / 3.5 mm needles, configured for circular knitting, or two sizes smaller than size needed to obtain gauge

US#6 / 4 mm needles, configured for circular knitting, or size needed to obtain gauge

Large-eyed sewing needle

Stitch marker

Gauge
20 sts and 20 rounds = 4 inches / 10 cm in pattern stitch, slightly stretched

Special Instructions
Slanted Columns Pattern (worked over 6 sts)

Rnd 1: K2, yo, k2, K2tog.

Rnd 2: Knit.

Repeat these 2 rnds.

Pattern
With smaller needles, cast on 84 (96, 108, 120) sts. Being careful not to twist, join to work in the round. Place marker at the beginning of the rnd.

Rnds 1 - 10: *K1, p1; repeat from * to end of rnd.

Change to larger needles and work in Slanted Columns Pattern for 5 (7, 7, 7) inches / 12.75 (17.75, 17.75, 17.75), or to desired length, ending after Rnd 2 of pattern.

Decrease top

Rnd 1: K4, k2tog; repeat from * to end of rnd. 70 (80, 90, 100) sts.

Rnd 2 (and all even rounds): Knit.

Rnd 3: *K3, k2tog; repeat from * to end of rnd. 56 (64, 72, 80) sts.

Rnd 5: *K2, k2tog; repeat from * to end of rnd. 42 (48, 54, 60) sts.

Rnd 7: *K1, k2tog; repeat from * to end of rnd. 28 (32, 36, 40) sts.

Rnd 9: *K2tog; repeat from * to end of rnd. 14 (16, 18, 20) sts.

Rnd 11: *K2tog; repeat from * to end of rnd. 7 (8, 9, 10) sts.

Finishing

Break yarn, leaving a 12 inch / 30.5 cm end. Thread yarn needle. Work yarn needle through remaining sts. Pull taut to close top of hat. Weave in ends.

Block.

Couldn't Be Easier

This is a simple hat pattern which makes it a great choice for community or charity knitting. Use a self-striping yarn or add stripes with multicolor yarns. It's a great stash buster.

Sizes
S (M, L, 1X)

Finished Measurements
Circumference 18 (20, 22, 24) inches / 45.75 (50.75, 55.75, 61) cm

Height to crown 6 (7, 7, 7) inches / 15.25 (17.75, 17.75, 17.75) cm

Total height 8 (9.25, 9.5, 9.75) inches / 20.25 (23.5, 24.25, 24.75) cm

Materials
Adriafil KNITCOL ART.KN (100% Merino Super wash; 137 yds per 50g skein); Color: Camo; 2 skeins

On model: Schachenmayr Regia 6Ply (75% Wool / 25% Polyamide; 410 yds per 150g skein); Color: Tweed 6967; 1 skein

US#5 / 3.75 mm needles, configured for circular knitting, or two sizes smaller than size needed to obtain gauge

US#7 / 4.5 mm needles, configured for circular knitting, or size needed to obtain gauge

Large-eyed sewing needle

Stitch marker

Gauge
20 sts and 28 rounds = 4 inches / 10 cm in stockinette stitch

Pattern
With smaller needles, cast 90 (100, 110, 120) sts. Being careful not to twist, join to work in the round. Place marker at the beginning of the rnd.

Rnds 1 - 10: *K1, p1; repeat from * to end of rnd.

Change to larger needles and work in stockinette st (k every rnd) until piece measures 6 (7, 7, 7) inches / 15.25 (17.75, 17.75, 17.75) cm, or desired length.

Decrease top

Size 1X only

Decrease Rnd: *K10, k2tog; repeat from * to end of rnd. (110 sts).

K 1 rnd.

Sizes L (1X) only

Decrease Rnd: *K9, k2tog; repeat from * to end of rnd. (100 sts).

Knit 1 rnd.

Sizes M (L, 1X) only

Decrease Rnd: *K8, k2tog; repeat from * to end of rnd. (90 sts).

Knit 1 rnd.

All Sizes

Rnd 1: *K7, k2tog; repeat from * to end of rnd. (80 sts).

Rnd 2 (and all even rnds): Knit.

Rnd 3: *K6, k2tog]; repeat from * to end of rnd. (70 sts).

Rnd 5: *K5, k2tog; repeat from * to end of rnd. (60 sts).

Rnd 7: *K4, k2tog; repeat from * to end of rnd. (50 sts).

Rnd 9: *K3, k2tog; repeat from * to end of rnd. (40 sts).

Rnd 11: *K2, k2tog; repeat from * to end of rnd. (30 sts).

Rnd 13: *K1, k2tog; repeat from * to end of rnd. (20 sts).

Rnd 14: *K2tog; repeat from * to end of rnd. (10 sts).

Finishing

Break yarn, leaving a 12 inch / 30.5 cm end. Thread yarn needle. Work yarn needle through remaining sts. Pull taut to close top of hat. Weave in ends.

Block.

Slam Hat

This hat starts with a simple 1x1 ribbing that develops into reverse stockinet panels. All the shaping is done in the panels. It is a quick and easy hat that appeals to many.

Sizes
S (M, L, 1X)

Finished Measurements
Circumference 18 (20, 22, 24) inches / 45.75 (50.75, 55.75, 61) cm

Height to crown 5.5 (6, 6.5, 7) inches / 14 (15.25, 16.5, 17.75) cm

Total height 7.5 (8.25, 9.25, 10) inches / 19 (21, 23.5, 25.5) cm

Materials
Blackberry Ridge Woolen Mill Medium Weight / Worsted Weight Traditional Colors (100% Wool; 230 yds per 4 oz skein); Color: Colonial Blue; 1 skein (On model – Color: Burgundy)

US#6 / 4 mm needles, configured for circular knitting, or two sizes smaller than size needed to obtain gauge.

US#8 / 6 mm needles, configured for circular knitting, or size needed to obtain gauge

Large-eyed sewing needle

Stitch marker

Gauge
16 sts and 24 rounds = 4 inches / 10 cm in stockinette stitch

Slam Hat Stitch Pattern
Rnd 1: K1, p1, k1, p6 (7, 8, 9).

Repeat Rnd 1

Pattern
With smaller needles, cast on 72 (80, 88, 96) sts. Being careful not to twist, join to work in the round. Place marker at the beginning of the rnd.

Rnds 1 - 10: *K1, p1; repeat from * to end of rnd.

Change to larger needles and work in Slam Hat Stitch Pattern until piece measures 5.5 (6, 6.5, 7) inches / 14 (15.25, 16.5, 17.75) cm, or desired length.

Decrease top

Size 1X only

Decrease Rnd: *K1, p1, ssk, p8; repeat from * to end of rnd. (88 sts).

Next Rnd: *K1, p1, k1, p8; repeat from * to end of rnd.

Sizes L (1X) only

Decrease Rnd: *K1, p1, ssk, p7; repeat from * to end of rnd. (80 sts).

Next Rnd: *K1, p1, k1, p7; repeat from * to end of rnd.

Sizes M (L, 1X) only

Decrease Rnd: *K1, p1, ssk, p6; repeat from * to end of rnd. (72 sts).

Next Rnd: *K1, p1, k1, p6; repeat from * to end of rnd.

All Sizes

Rnd 1: *K1, p1, ssk, p5; repeat from * to end of rnd. (64 sts).

Rnd 2 (and all even rnds): Work sts as they appear.

Rnd 3: *K1, p1, ssk, p4; repeat from * to end of rnd. (56 sts).

Rnd 5: *K1, p1, ssk, p3; repeat from * to end of rnd. (48 sts).

Rnd 7: *K1, p1, ssk, p2; repeat from *

to end of rnd. (40 sts).

Rnd 9: *K1, p1, ssk, p1; repeat from * to end of rnd. (32 sts).

Rnd 11: *Ssk, p1; repeat from * to end of rnd. (16 sts).

Rnd 12: *Ssk; repeat from * to end of rnd. (8 sts).

Finishing

Break yarn, leaving a 12 inch / 30.5 cm end. Thread yarn needle. Work yarn needle through remaining sts. Pull taut to close top of hat. Weave in ends.

Block.

Latvian Cloche

The Latvian two-color braid on this hat is simple to do. As you purl with two colors, you'll see the lovely braid emerge as you bring one yarn over the other and then under the other on the next round. The same technique is used for the border of the large flower. Find a great button for the flower's center. Wear your hat with the flower anywhere that suits your fancy.

Sizes
S (M, L)

Finished Measurements
Circumference 18 (20, 22) inches / 45.75 (50.75, 55.75) cm

Height to crown 5.5 (6, 6.5, 7) inches / 14 (15.25, 16.5) cm

Total height 7.5 (8.25, 9.25, 10) inches / 19 (21, 23.5) cm

Materials
Blackberry Ridge Woolen Mill Medium Weight / Worsted Weight Traditional Colors Yarn (100% Wool; 230 yds per 4 oz skein); Colors: MC Colonial Blue; 1 skein. CC1 Light Blue; 100 yds. CC2 Aster; 100 yds.

US#6 / 4 mm needles, configured for circular knitting, or two sizes smaller than size needed to obtain gauge.

US#8 / 6 mm needles, configured for circular knitting, or size needed to obtain gauge

Large-eyed sewing needle

Stitch marker

1 button (7/8" to 1 inch in diameter)

Gauge
16 sts and 22 rounds = 4 inches / 10cm in stockinette stitch

Special Instructions
Latvian Braid

Rnd 1: *K1 with CC1, K1 with CC2; repeat from * around. Bring both CC1 and CC2 to front of work so you're ready to purl on next rnd

Rnd 2: P1 in CC1, *bring CC2 over CC1 and p1, bring CC1 over CC2 and p1; repeat from *around, end by bringing CC2 over CC1 and p1.

Rnd 3: P1 in CC1, *bring CC2 under CC1 and p1, bring CC1 under CC2 and p1; repeat from * around, end by bringing CC2 under CC1 and p1.

Pattern

Using smaller needles and MC, cast on 144 (160, 176) sts. Being careful not to twist, join to work in the round. Place marker at the beginning of the rnd.

Rnd 1: Knit.

Rnd 2: *K2tog; repeat from * around. 72 (80, 88) sts.

Drop MC but do not break. Let it hang behind your work until you're ready to use it again.

Attach CC1 and CC2.

Work 3 rnds of Latvian Braid.

Bring CC1 and CC2 to back of work. Break CC1 and CC2.

Continue working with MC. Using larger needles, knit every round until piece measures, 6, (8, 8) inches / 15.25 (20.25, 20.25) cm, or desired height.

Decrease top

Size L only

Dec Rnd: *K9, k2tog; repeat from * around. 80 sts.

Next Rnd: Knit.

Sizes M (L) only

Dec Rnd: *K8, k2tog; repeat from * around. 72 sts.

Next Rnd: Knit.

All sizes

Rnd 1: *K7, k2tog; repeat from * around. (64 sts)

Rnd 2: Knit.

Rnd 3: *K6, k2tog; repeat from * around. (56 sts)

Rnd 4: Knit.

Rnd 5: *K5, k2tog; repeat from * around. (48 sts)

Rnd 6: Knit.

Rnd 7: *K4, k2tog; repeat from * around. (40 sts)

Rnd 8: *K3, k2tog; repeat from * around. (32 sts)

Rnd 9: *K2, k2tog; repeat from * around. (24 sts)

Rnd 10: *K1, k2tog; repeat from * around. (16 sts)

Rnd 11: *K2tog; repeat from * around. (8 sts)

Finishing

Break yarn, leaving a 12 inch / 30.5 cm end. Thread yarn needle. Work yarn needle through remaining sts. Pull taut to close top of hat. Weave in ends.

Flower

With smaller needles and MC, cast on 84 sts. Being careful not to twist, join to work in the round. Place marker at the beginning of the rnd.

Rnds 1-3: Knit.

Rnd 4: Purl.

Rnd 5: Knit.

Rnd 6: Purl.

Rnd 7: Knit.

Drop MC but do not break. Let it hang behind your work until you're ready to use it again.

Rnds 8 - 10: With CC1 and CC2. work Latvian Braid.

Bring CC1 and CC2 to back of work. Break CC1 and CC2.

Rnds 11: With MC, knit.

Rnd 12: Purl.

Rnds 13 - 15: Knit.

Rnd 16: *K1, k2tog; repeat from * around. 56 sts.

Rnd 17: Knit.

Rnd 18: *K2tog; repeat from * around. 28 sts.

Break yarn, leaving a 12 inch / 30.5 cm end. Thread yarn needle. Work yarn needle through remaining sts. Pull taut to close flower. Place flower on hat. Sew button to middle of flower and through the all thicknesses to secure flower to hat. Weave in ends and block.

Nordic Shimmer

Using a self-striping yarn, two separate balls are paired so that the colors will contrast. The color values vary so there are places of high and low contrast. This hat would also be fun to knit in two solid colors or with two gradients. Corrugated rib is used for the bottom band and for the crown. The crown has a unique squared shaping.

Sizes
S (M, L, 1X)

Finished Measurements
Circumference 18 (21, 22.5, 24) inches / 45.75 (53.25, 57.25, 61) cm

Height to crown 5.5 (6.75, 6.75, 6.75) inches / 14 (17.25, 17.25, 17.25) cm

Total height 8 (9, 9.5, 10) inches / 20 (23, 24, 25.5) cm

Materials
Knit One Crochet Too Paint Box (100% Wool; 197 yds per 100g skein); Color: 9; 2 skeins

US#6 / 4 mm needles, configured for circular knitting, or two sizes smaller than size needed to obtain gauge.

US#8 / 6 mm needles, configured for circular knitting, or size needed to obtain gauge

Large-eyed sewing needle

Stitch marker

Gauge
16 sts and 24 rounds = 4 inches / 10 cm in color pattern

Special Instructions
Two Color cast on

Using MC as the yarn that goes over the needle, and CC as the yarn that wraps around the thumb and traps the stitch, work long tail cast on.

Corrugated rib

*With MC, k2, leave MC to back of work; bring CC to front, p2, bring CC to back of work; repeat from * to end of rnd.

Pattern
Designate one skein as MC and one skein as CC. Starting at a point in each skein with a color that contrasts with the starting color in the other skein, set up to use the long tail cast on.

With smaller needles, using the Two Color method, cast on 72 (84, 90, 96) sts as follows:

Using MC as the yarn that goes over the needle, and CC as the yarn that wraps around the thumb and traps the stitch, work long tail cast on.

Row 1: Work 1 row of corrugated ribbing.

Being careful not to twist, join to work in the round, placing a marker at the beginning of the rnd.

Rnds 2 - 10: Work corrugated ribbing.

Rnd 11: With MC, knit.

Rnd 12: With CC, purl.

Rnd 13: With MC, knit.

Rnd 14: Change to larger needles, and with MC, knit.

Size S only: Work Nordic Shimmer Main Chart starting at Rnd 3, 12 times around.

Sizes M (L, 1X): Work Nordic Shimmer Main Chart starting at Rnd 1, 14 (15, 16) times around.

Work until 26 (29, 29, 29) rnds of Nordic Shimmer Main Chart have been completed.

Next Rnd: With MC, knit.

Decrease Rnd: Decrease 0 (4, 2, 0) sts evenly on the second rnd. 72 (80, 88, 96) sts.

Following Rnd: With CC, purl.

Begin top decrease

Follow Nordic Shimmer Crown Chart for your size.

Finishing

Break yarn, leaving a 12 inch / 30.5 cm end. Thread yarn needle. Work yarn needle through remaining sts. Pull taut to close top of hat. Weave in ends.

Block.

Main Chart

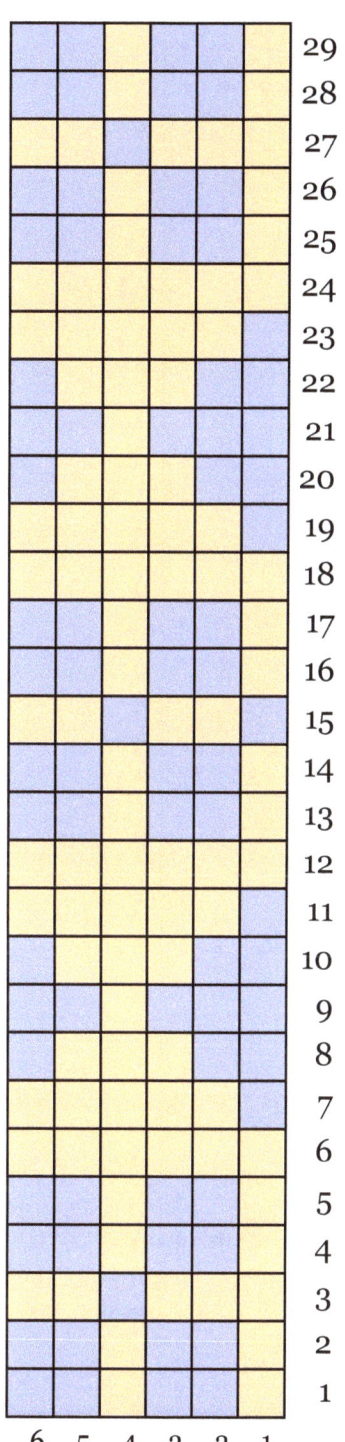

☐	No stitch
☐ MC	MC
☐ CC	CC
●	Purl
�╲	Ssk
⦸	P2tog
木	Sl1, k2tog, psso

72-st Crown Chart

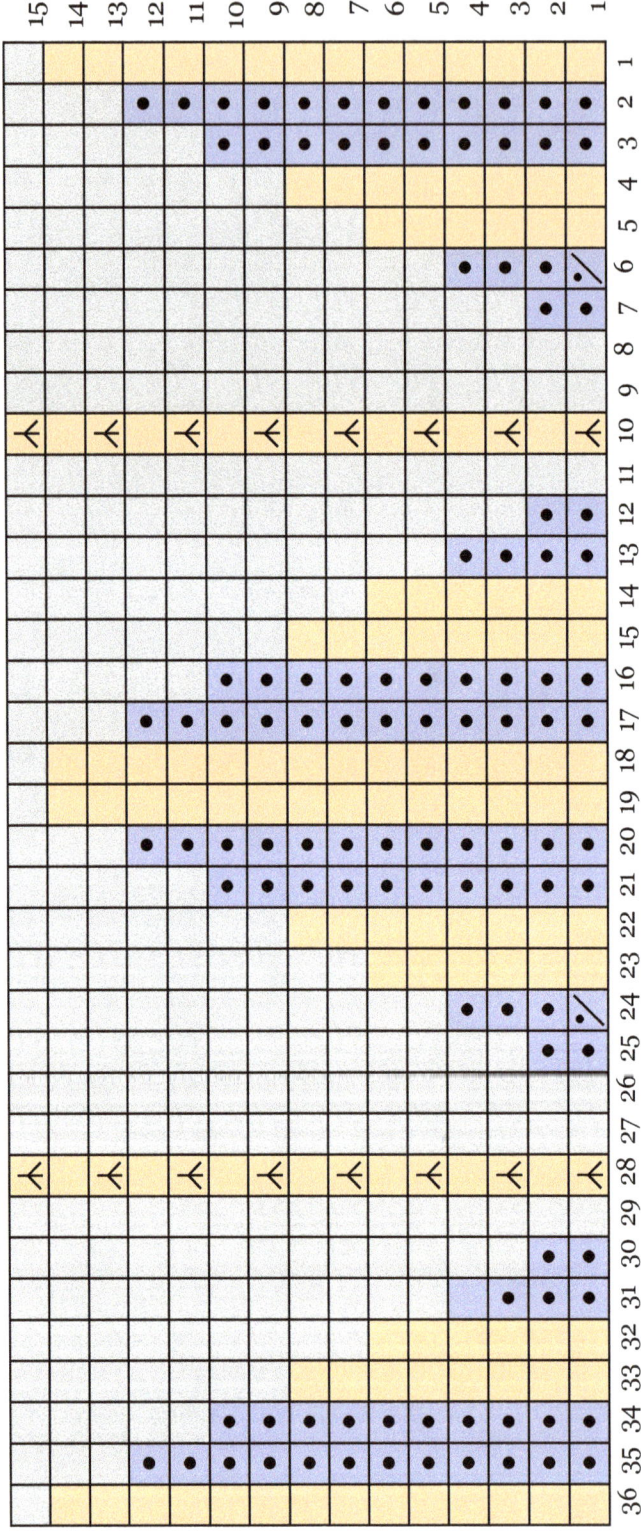

84

84-st Crown Chart

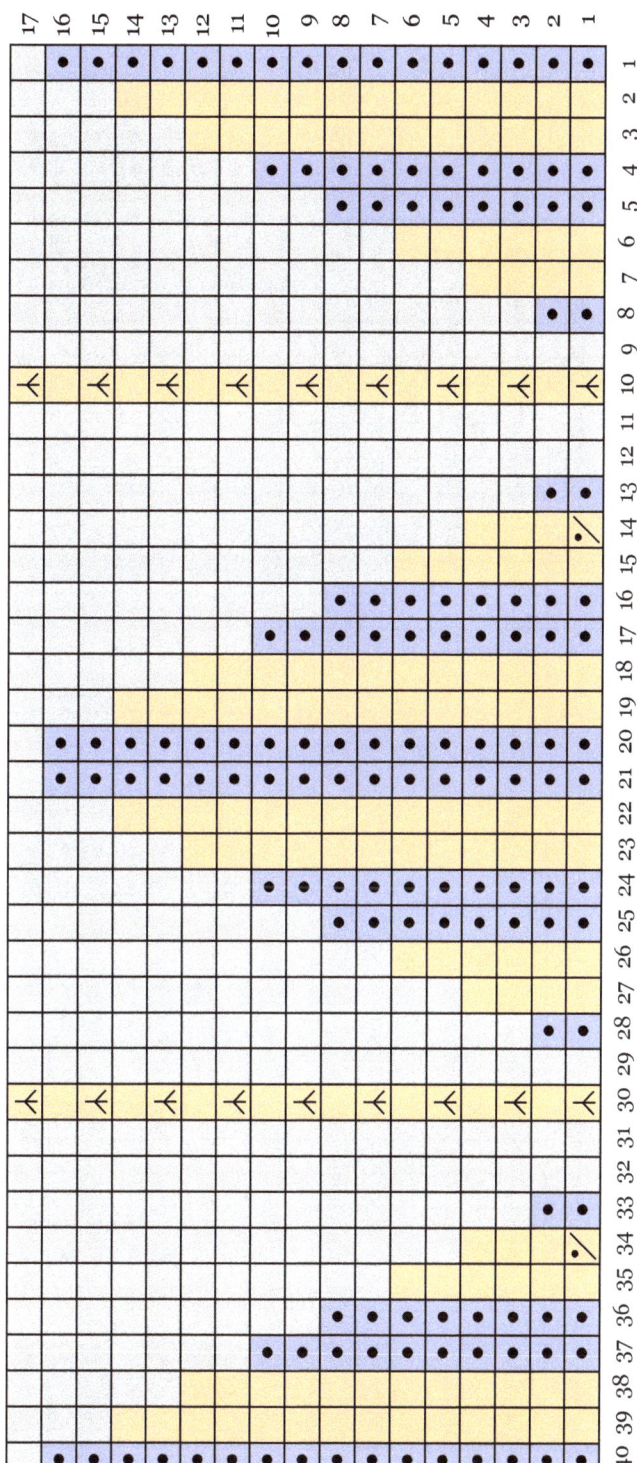

88-st Crown Chart

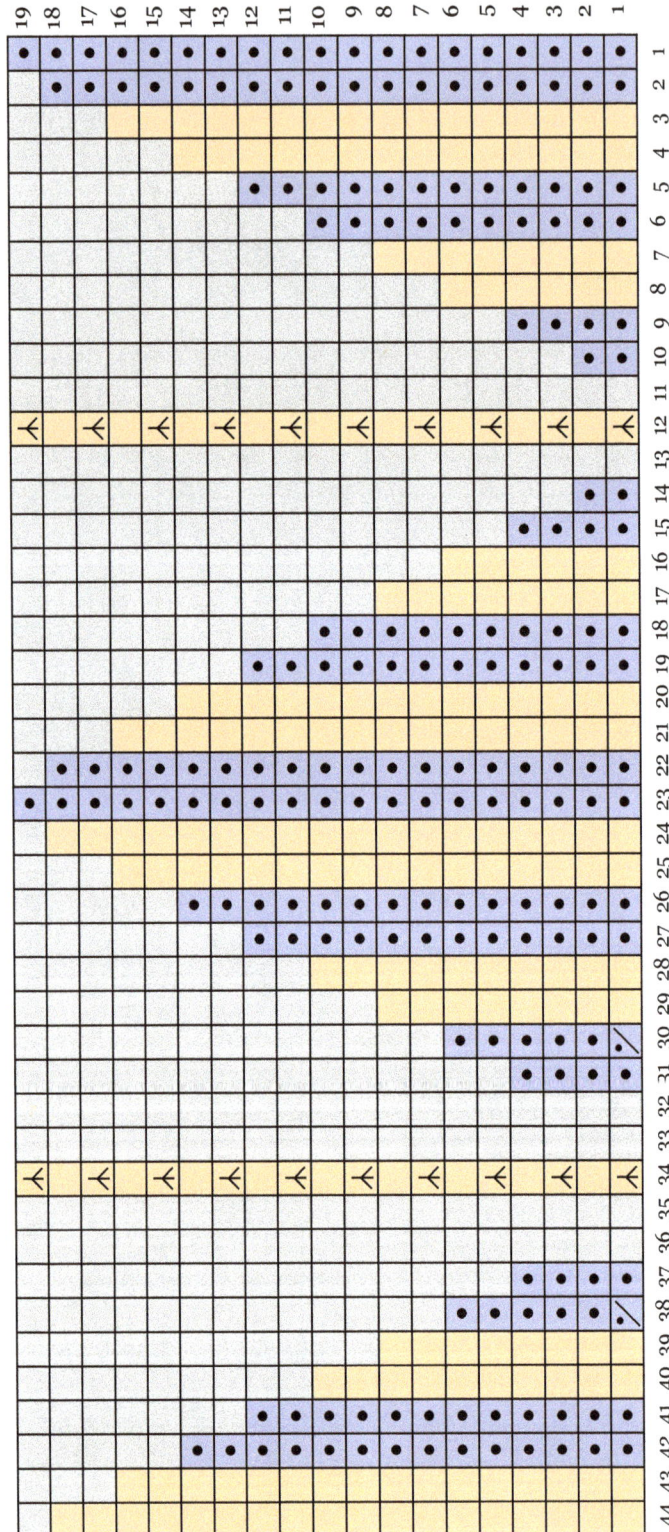

96-st Crown Chart

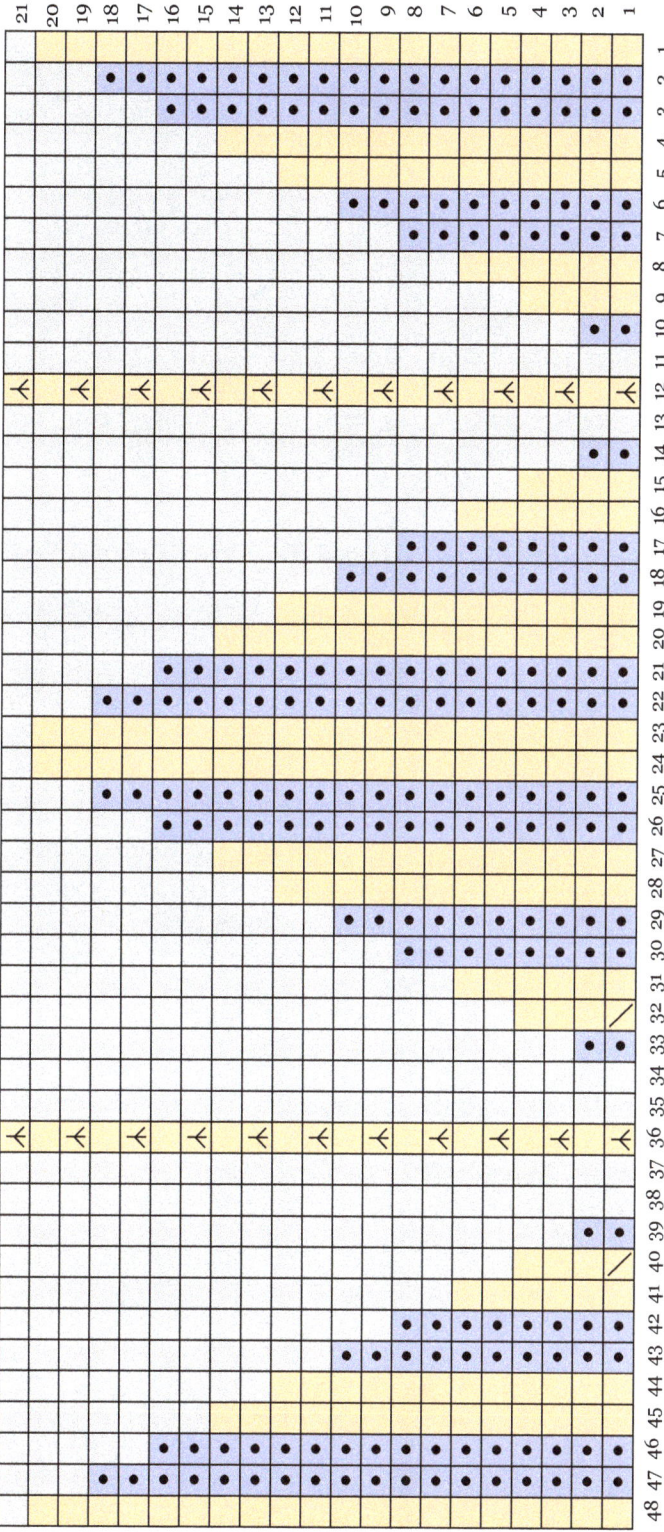

Weird Warm Hat

Back and forth short-row shaping produces this hat's helmet shape. The work is then rejoined for working in the round to complete the hat. Although a weird shape, it is a comfortable and warm hat and surprisingly flattering.

Size
One size

Finished Measurements
Circumference 22 inches / 55.75 cm

Length 19.5 inches / 49.5 cm

Materials
Knit One Crochet Too Paint Box (100% Wool; 197 yds per 100g skein); Color: 9; 2 skeins

US#6 / 4 mm needles, configured for circular knitting, or two sizes smaller than size needed to obtain gauge.

US#8 / 6 mm needles, configured for circular knitting, or size needed to obtain gauge

Large-eyed sewing needle

Stitch marker

Gauge
16 sts and 16 rounds = 4 inches /10 cm in color pattern

Special Instructions
Two color cast on

Using MC as the yarn that goes over the needle, and CC as the yarn that wraps around the thumb and traps the stitch, work long tail cast on.

Pattern
With smaller needles, and starting at a point in each skein with a color that contrasts with the starting color in the other skein, cast on 100 sts using Two Color Cast On method.

Being careful not to twist, join to work in the round, placing a marker at the beginning of the rnd.

Rnd 1: With MC, knit.

Rnd 2: With MC, purl.

Rnd 3: With CC, knit.

Rnd 4: With CC, purl.

Rnd 5: With MC, knit.

Rnd 6: With CC, purl.

Remove marker.

Change to larger needles and begin

working back and forth.

Row 7: Follow Row 1 of Weird Warm Chart A, working in color pattern across first 28 sts. Turn.

Row 8: Follow Row 2 of Weird Warm Chart A over next 29 sts. Turn.

Continue in this manner, keeping the color pattern correct, adding one st per row until you have 71 sts worked. Turn.

Replace marker to designate new start of rnd.

Next Rnd: Working in the rnd, complete all rnds of Weird Warm Chart B.

To make the hat taller, or shorter, work fewer or more rnds of Chart B. Please note that ending after a partial chart repeat will mean that the crown chart will not line up. If you're comfortable with the pattern however, it is quite easy to continue in pattern as set, working the decreases in the places set in the crown chart.

Decrease top by working Weird Warm Chart C.

Finishing

Break yarn, leaving a 12 inch / 30.5 cm end. Thread yarn needle. Work yarn needle through remaining sts. Pull taut to close top of hat. Weave in ends.

Block. Make a tassel and attach to top of hat.

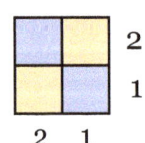

No stitch

MC

CC

Ssk

Chart C

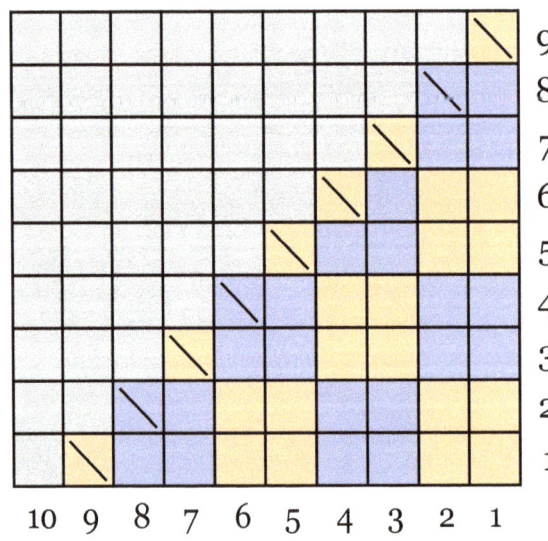

10 9 8 7 6 5 4 3 2 1

Chart A

Chart B

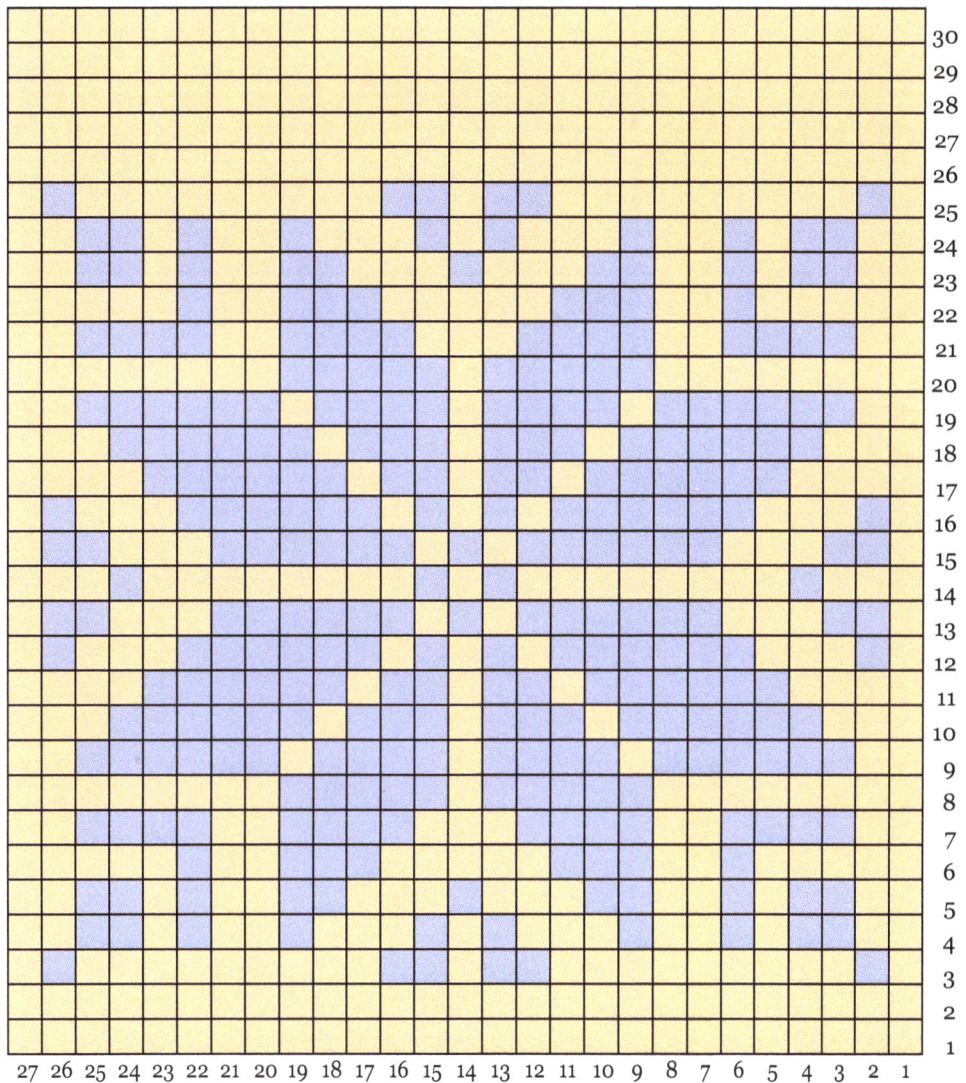

Winter Stars

In this hat, a traditional small star pattern is flanked by two sweet borders. The crown is knit without color-work. Sporting a basic shape and popular design, this hat will appeal to many. Try adding more colors or using a highly contrasting speckled yarn for the main color.

Sizes
S (M, L, 1X)

Finished Measurements
Circumference 18 (21.25, 21.25, 24) inches / 45.75 (54, 54, 61) cm

Height to crown 5.5 (6.25, 6.75, 7.25) inches / 14 (15.75, 17, 18.5) cm

Total height 8 (8.75, 9.25, 9.75) inches / 20 (22.5, 23.5, 24.5) cm

Materials
Blackberry Ridge Woolen Mill Medium Weight/Worsted Weight Traditional Colors Yarn (100% Wool; 230 yds per 4 oz skein); Colors: MC Light Blue; 1 skein. CC Aster; 1 skein.

US#5 / 3.75 mm needles, configured for circular knitting, or two sizes smaller than size needed to obtain gauge.

US#7 / 4.5 mm needles, configured for circular knitting, or size needed to obtain gauge

Large-eyed sewing needle

Stitch marker

Gauge
18 sts and 26 rounds = 4 inches / 10 cm in stockinette stitch

Special Instructions
Two Color Cast On

Use MC as the yarn that goes over the needle, and CC as the yarn that wraps around the thumb and traps the stitch, work long tail cast on.

Pattern
With smaller needles, and using Two Color Cast On method, cast on 84 (90, 96, 102) sts. Leave a 12 inch / 30.5 cm tail for sewing up later.

Rows 1 and 2: With MC, knit.

Rows 3 - 10: With CC, knit.

Change to larger needles, and join to work in the round, placing a marker at start of rnd.

With MC, knit 1 (3, 3, 3) rnds, increasing 0 (6, 0, 6) sts evenly spaced on the second rnd. 84 (96, 96, 108) sts.

Work all rnds of Winter Stars Chart.

With MC, knit 5 (8, 11, 14) rnds, or to desired height.

Decrease top

Rnd 1: *K10, ssk; repeat from * to end of rnd. 77 (88, 88, 99) sts.

Rnd 2: Knit.

Rnd 3: *K9, ssk; repeat from * to end of rnd.

Rnd 4: Knit.

Rnd 5: *K8, ssk; repeat from * to end of rnd.

Rnd 6: Knit.

Rnd 7: *K7, ssk; repeat from * to end of rnd.

Rnd 8: Knit.

Rnd 9: *K6, ssk; repeat from * to end of rnd.

Rnd 10: Knit.

Rnd 11: *K5, ssk; repeat from * to end of rnd.

Rnd 12: Knit.

Rnd 13: *K4, ssk; repeat from * to end of rnd.

Rnd 14: *K3, ssk; repeat from * to end of rnd.

Rnd 15: *K2, ssk; repeat from * to end of rnd.

Rnd 16: *K1, ssk; repeat from * to end of rnd.

Rnd 17: *Ssk; repeat from * to end of rnd. 7 (8, 8, 9) sts.

Finishing

Break yarn, leaving a 12 inch / 30.5 cm end. Thread yarn needle. Work yarn needle through remaining sts. Pull taut to close top of hat. Weave in ends.

Using cast on tail, neatly seam garter st band. Weave in ends.

Block.

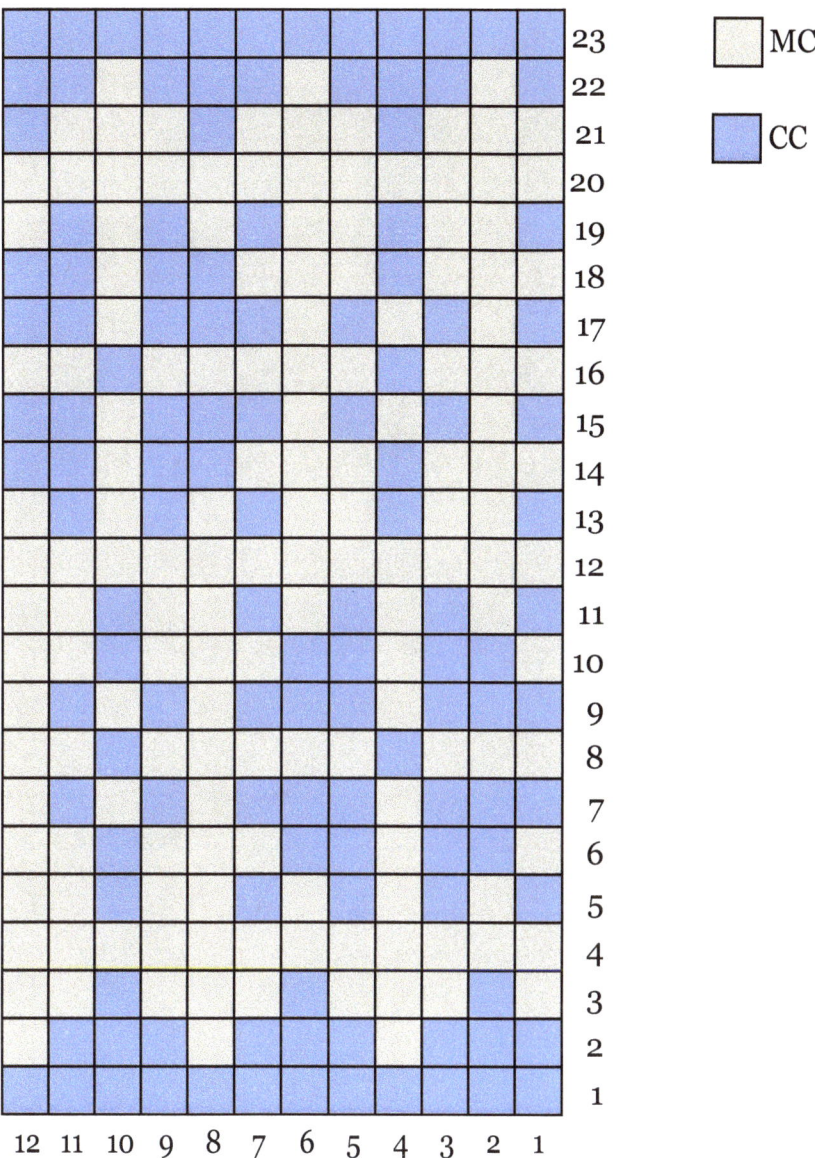

MC

CC

Fancy Hug Beanie

Paired cables form the ribbing on this hat. When the cable crosses are abandoned, the knit and purl pattern is maintained. Quickly knit in an Aran weight yarn, this hat has enough pattern work to make the knitting interesting.

Sizes
S (M, L, 1X)

Finished Measurements
Circumference 18 (20, 22, 24) inches / 45.5 (51, 56, 61) cm

Height to crown 5 (5, 5.75, 6) inches / 12.8 (12.8, 14.5, 15) cm

Total height 7 (7, 7.75, 8) inches / 18 (18, 19.5, 20) cm

Materials
Noro Kama Aran Weight Yarn (26% Wool 28% Silk 25% Alpaca 12% Angora; 82 yds per 50 gm skein); Color: 6; 1 (2, 2, 2) skeins.

skein.

US#8/ 5 mm needles, configured for circular knitting, or size needed to obtain gauge.

Large-eyed sewing needle

Stitch marker

Gauge
16 sts and 22 rounds = 4 inches / 10 cm in stitch pattern

Pattern
Cast on 72 (80, 88, 96) sts. Being careful not to twist, join to work in the round, placing a marker at the beginning of the rnd.

Rnds 1 - 3: *K8, p1 (2, 3, 4); repeat from * around.

Rnd 4: *2/2 RC, 2/2 LC, p1 (2, 3, 4); repeat from * around.

Rnds 5 - 16: Repeat Rnds 1 - 4 three (3) times.

Rnds 17 - 26 (26, 28, 30): *K8, p1 (2, 3, 4); repeat from * around.

To lengthen before crown, work more repeats of Rnd 17.

To shorten before crown, work less repeats of Rnd 17.

Decrease top

Size 1X only

Rnd 1: K1, *k6, ssk, p2, k2tog; repeat from * around, ending with k2tog last st of rnd with first st of next rnd. Move marker to after this st. 80 sts.

Rnd 2: *K8, p2; repeat from * to end of rnd.

Rnd 3: *K6, ssk, k2tog; repeat around. 64 sts.

Rnd 4: Knit.

Sizes L only

Rnd 1: K1, *k6, ssk, p1, k2tog; repeat from * around, ending k2tog last st of with first st of next rnd. Move marker to after this st. 72 sts.

Rnd 2: *K8, p1; repeat from * to end of rnd.

Rnd 3: *K7, ssk; repeat from * around. 64 sts.

Rnd 4: Knit.

Size M only

Rnd 1: K1, *k6, ssk, k2tog; repeat from * around, ending k2tog last st of red with first st of next rnd. Move marker to after this st. 64 sts.

Rnd 2: Knit.

Size S only

Rnd 1: *K7, ssk; repeat from * around. 64 sts.

Rnd 2: Knit.

All sizes

Rnd 1: *K6, k2tog; repeat from * to end of rnd. 56 sts.

Rnd 2: Knit.

Rnd 3: *K5, k2tog; repeat from * to end of rnd. 48 sts.

Rnd 4: Knit.

Rnd 5: *K4, k2tog; repeat from * to end of rnd. 40 sts.

Rnd 6: Knit.

Rnd 7: *K3, k2tog; repeat from * to end of rnd. 32 sts.

Rnd 8: *2/2 RC, 2/2 LC; repeat from * to end of round. 32 sts.

Rnd 9: *K2, k2tog; repeat from * to end of rnd. 24 sts.

Rnd 10: *K1, k2tog; repeat from * to end of rnd. 16 sts.

Rnd 11: *K2tog; repeat from * to end of rnd. 8 sts.

Finishing

Break yarn, leaving a 12 inch / 30.5 cm end. Thread yarn needle. Work yarn needle through remaining sts. Pull taut to close top of hat. Weave in ends.

Block.

Stop the Purl

Quick to knit in an Aran weight yarn, this hat begins with a simple 2x2 ribbing. For the body of the hat, every other purl farrow is stopped. Evenly spaced decreasing on every other round completes the crown.

Sizes
S (M, L, 1X)

Finished Measurements
Circumference 18.25 (20.5, 22.75, 25) inches / 46.5 (52, 57.75, 63.5) cm

Height to crown 4 (6, 7, 7) inches / 10 (15.25, 17.75, 17.75) cm

Total height 6.5 (7.5, 8.5, 8.5) inches / 16.5 (19, 21.5, 21.5) cm

Materials
Noro Kama Aran Weight Yarn (26% Wool 28% Silk 25% Alpaca 12% Angora; 82 yds per 50 gm skein); Color: 6; 1 (2, 2, 2) skeins.

US#6 / 4.25 mm needles, or two sizes smaller than size needed to obtain gauge

US#8/ 5 mm needles, configured for circular knitting, or size needed to obtain gauge.

Large-eyed sewing needle

Stitch marker

Gauge
14 sts and 22 rounds = 4 inches / 10 cm in stockinette stitch

Pattern
With smaller needles, cast on 64 (72, 80, 88) sts. Being careful not to twist, join to work in the round, placing a marker at the beginning of the rnd.

Rnds 1 - 10: *K2, p2; repeat from * to end of rnd.

Change to larger needles.

Rnd 11: *K6, p2; repeat from * to end of rnd.

Repeat Rnd 11 until piece measures 4 (5, 6, 6) inches / 10 (12.75, 15, 15) cm.

To increase or decrease height, work fewer or more repeats of Rnd 11.

Decrease top

Rnd 1: K5, *ssk, k2tog, k4; repeat from * around, ending k2tog last st of rnd with first st of next rnd. Move marker to after this st. 48 (54, 60, 66) sts.

Rnd 2: Knit.

Rnd 3: *K4, k2tog; repeat from * to end of rnd. 40 (45, 50, 55) sts.

Rnd 4: Knit.

Rnd 5: *K3, k2tog; repeat from * to end of rnd. 32 (36, 40, 44) sts.

Rnd 6: Knit.

Rnd 7: *K2, k2tog; repeat from * to end of rnd. 24 (27, 30, 33) sts.

Rnd 8: Knit.

Rnd 9: *K1, k2tog; repeat from * to end of rnd. 16 (18, 20, 22) sts.

Rnd 10: Knit.

Rnd 11: *K2tog; repeat from * to end of rnd. 8 (9, 10, 11) sts.

Finishing

Break yarn, leaving a 12 inch / 30.5 cm end. Thread yarn needle. Work yarn needle through remaining sts. Pull taut to close top of hat. Weave in ends.

Block.

Wood Stove Beanie

Reminiscent of a pot belly wood stove, this hat begins with an antler-type cable for the ribbing. The cable pattern then alternates around the hat and is abandoned at the crown.

Sizes
M (1X)

Finished Measurements
Circumference 19 (23) inches / 48.25 (58.5) cm

Height to crown 7 (8.5) inches / 17.75 (21.5) cm

Total height 9 (10.5) inches / 22.75 (26.75) cm

Materials
Noro Kama Aran Weight Yarn (26% Wool 28% Silk 25% Alpaca 12% Angora; 82 yds per 50 gm skein); Color: 6; 1 (2, 2, 2) skeins.

US#8/ 5 mm needles, configured for circular knitting, or size needed to obtain gauge.

Large-eyed sewing needle

Stitch marker

Gauge
17 sts and 23 rnds = 4 inches / 10 cm in pattern stitch

Pattern
Cast on 80 (96) sts. Being careful not to twist, join to work in the round, placing marker at the beginning of the rnd.

Rnd 1: *K6, p2; repeat from * around.

Rnd 2: *1/2 RC, 1/2 LC, p2; repeat from * around.

Rnds 3 - 12: Work first 2 rnds five (5) more times.

Rnd 13: As Rnd 1.

Rnds 14, 16, 18: *1/2 RC, 1/2 LC, p2, k6, p2; repeat from * around.

Rnds 15, 17, 19: *K6, p2; repeat from * around.

Rnds 20, 22, 24: *K6, p2, 1/2 RC, 1/2 LC, p2; repeat from * around.

Rnds 21, 23, 25: *K6, p2; repeat from * around.

Rnds 26, 28, 30: *1/2 RC, 1/2 LC, p2, K6, p2; repeat from * around.

Rnds 27, 29, 31: *K6, p2; repeat from * around.

Size L only

Repeat Rnds 20 - 26.

All Sizes

Knit 2 rnds.

To adjust height to crown, work fewer rnds in pattern, or add more plain knit rnds after pattern has been completed.

Decrease top

Rnd 1: K1, *k4, ssk, k2tog; repeat from * around ending with k2tog last st of rnd with first st of next rnd. Move marker to after this st. 60 (72) sts.

Rnd 2 and all even rnds: Knit.

Rnd 3: *K4, k2tog; repeat from * around. 50 (60) sts.

Rnd 5: *K3, k2tog; repeat from * around. 40 (48) sts.

Rnd 7: *K2, k2tog; repeat from * around. 30 (36) sts.

Rnd 9: *K1, k2tog; repeat from * around. 20 (24) sts.

Rnd 11: *K2tog; repeat from * around. 10 (12) sts.

Rnd 13: *K2tog; repeat from * around. 5 (6) sts.

Rnd 14: Knit.

Finishing

Break yarn, leaving a 12 inch end. Thread yarn needle. Work yarn needle through remaining sts. Pull taut to close top of hat. Weave in ends.

Block.

Capitol Square

Fun to knit with a self-striping yarn with long color changes, this hat uses alternating bands of stockinette and seed stitch for textural interest. The crown is shaped by double decreases at four points forming a square.

Sizes
S (M, L, 1X)

Finished Measurements
Circumference 17.75 (19.5, 21.5, 23.25) inches / 45 (49.5, 54.5, 59) cm

Height to crown 5.25 inches / 13.25 cm

Total height 8.5 (8.5, 8.75, 9) inches / 21.5 (21.5, 22.25, 23) cm

Materials
Noro Silk Garden (45% Mohair, 45% Silk, 10% Wool; 110 yds per 50g skein); Color: 395; 2 skeins

US#6 / 4.25 mm needles, or two sizes smaller than size needed to obtain gauge

US#8/ 5 mm needles, configured for circular knitting, or size needed to obtain gauge.

Large-eyed sewing needle

Stitch marker

Gauge
18 sts and 25 rounds = 4 inches / 10 cm in pattern

Pattern
With smaller needles, cast on 80 (88, 96, 104) sts, leaving a 12 inch / 30.5 cm end for sewing up later.

Rows 1 - 10: Knit.

Change to larger needles, and join to work in the round, placing a marker at the beginning of the rnd.

Rnds 11 - 14: Knit.

Rnd 15: *K1, p1; repeat from * to end of rnd.

Rnd 16: *P1, k1; repeat from * to end of rnd.

Rnds 17 - 34: Work Rnds 11 - 16 three (3) times.

Rnds 35 and 36: Knit.

To make the hat taller or shorter, work fewer or more repeats of Rnds 11 - 16, then work Rnds 35 and 36.

Decrease top

Rnd 37: *K8 (9, 10, 11), p3tog, k9, (10, 11, 12); repeat from * to end of rnd. 72 (80, 88, 96) sts.

Rnd 38: *K1, p1; repeat from * to

end of rnd.

Rnd 39: *P1, k1; repeat from * to end of rnd.

Rnd 40: *K7 (8, 9, 10, p3tog, k8, (9, 10, 11); repeat from * to end of rnd. 64 (72, 80, 88) sts.

Rnd 41: Knit.

Rnd 42: *K6 (7, 8, 9), p3tog, k7, (8, 9, 10); repeat from * to end of rnd. 56 (64, 72, 80) sts.

Rnd 43: Knit.

Rnd 44: *K5 (6, 7, 8), p3tog, k6, (7, 8, 9; repeat from * to end of rnd. 48 (56, 64, 72) sts.

Rnd 45: *K1, p1; repeat from * to end of rnd.

Rnd 46: *P1, k1; repeat from * to end of rnd.

Rnd 47: *K4 (5, 6, 7), p3tog, k5, (6, 7, 8); repeat from * to end of rnd. 40 (48, 56, 64) sts.

Rnd 48: Knit.

Rnd 49: *K3 (4, 5, 6), p3tog, k4 (5, 6, 7); repeat from * to end of rnd. 32 (40, 48, 56) sts.

Rnd 50: *K1, p1; repeat from * to end of rnd.

Rnd 51: *P1, k1; repeat from * to end of rnd.

Rnd 52: *K2 (3, 4, 5), p3tog, k3 (4, 5, 6); repeat from * to end of rnd. 24 (32, 40, 48) sts.

Rnd 53: Knit.

Rnd 54: *K1 (2,3, 4), p3tog, k2 (3, 4, 5); repeat from * to end of rnd. 16 (24, 32, 40) sts.

Rnd 55: *K1, p1; repeat from * to end of rnd.

Rnd 56: *P1, k1; repeat from * to end of rnd.

Rnd 57: *K0 (1, 2, 3), p3tog, k1 (2, 3, 4); repeat from * to end of rnd. 8, (16, 24, 32) sts.

Size M (L, 1X) only

Rnd 58: *K0 (1, 2), p3tog, k1, (2, 3); repeat from * to end of rnd. 8 (16, 24) sts.

Size L (1X) only

Rnd 59: *K0 (1), p3tog, k1 (2); repeat from * to end of rnd. 8 (16) sts.

Size 1X only

Rnd 60: *P3tog, k1; repeat from * to end of rnd. 4 sts.

Finishing

Break yarn, leaving a 12 inch / 30.5 cm end. Thread yarn needle. Work yarn needle through remaining sts. Pull taut to close top of hat.

Using tail from cast on, neatly seam garter st band. Weave in ends.

Block.

Equine Cloche

Starting with an antler cable ribbing and moving onto thick horseshoe cables, this hat design would also be suitable for a solid color, a tonal, a speckled, or a gradient dyed yarn.

Sizes
S (M, L, 1X)

Finished Measurements
Circumference 19 (20.25, 21.75, 23.25) inches 18 (20, 21.5, 23) inches

Height to crown 6 (6.25, 6.5, 7) inches / 15.25 (16, 16.5, 17.25) cm (excluding 0.75 inch / 1.75 cm garter band)

Total height 8.25 (8.5, 8.75, 9.25) inches / 21 (21.5, 22.25, 23.5) cm

Materials
Noro Silk Garden (45% Mohair, 45% Silk, 10% Wool; 110 yds per 50g skein); Color: 395; 2 skeins

US#6 / 4.25 mm needles, or two sizes smaller than size needed to obtain gauge

US#8/ 5 mm needles, configured for circular knitting, or size needed to obtain gauge.

Large-eyed sewing needle

Stitch marker

Gauge
20 sts and 24 rounds = 4 inches / 10 cm in antler cable pattern

Pattern
With larger needles, cast on 90 (99, 108, 1117) sts. Being careful not to twist, join to work in the round, placing a marker at the beginning of the rnd.

Rnds 1 - 3: Knit.

Rnd 4: *3/1RC, k1, 1/3LC; repeat from * around.

Rnds 5 - 7: Knit.

Repeat last Rnds 4 - 7 twice more.

Rnds 16 - 18: Knit.

Rnd 19: [5/5RC, 5/5LC, k10 (13, 16, 19)]
3 times.

Rnds 20 - 29: Knit.

Rnds 30 - 36 (38, 40, 40): Repeat Rnds 19 - 25 (27, 29, 29)

Size 1X only

Knit 2 rnds.

To change the height of the hat, work more or fewer rnds of pattern.

Decrease top:

Rnd 1: *K7, k2tog; repeat from * to end of rnd. 80 (88, 96, 104) sts.

Rnd 2 (and all even rnds): Knit.

Rnd 3: *K6, k2tog; repeat from * to end of rnd. 70 (77, 84, 91) sts.

Rnd 5: *K5, k2tog; repeat from * to end of rnd. 60 (66, 72, 78) sts.

Rnd 7: *K4, k2tog; repeat from * to end of rnd. 50 (55, 60, 65) sts.

Rnd 9: *K3, k2tog; repeat from * to end of rnd. 40 (44, 48, 52) sts.

Rnd 11: *K2, k2tog; repeat from * to end of rnd. 30 (33, 36, 39) sts.

Rnd 13: *K1, k2tog; repeat from * to end of rnd. 20 (22, 24, 26) sts.

Rnd 15: *K2tog, repeat from * to end of rnd. 10 (11, 12, 13) sts.

Finishing

Break yarn, leaving a 12 inch / 30.5 cm end. Thread yarn needle. Work yarn needle through remaining sts. Pull taut to close top of hat. Weave in ends.

With smaller needles, pick up and knit 90(99, 108, 117) sts across cast on edge.

Rnd 1: Knit.

Rnd 2: Purl.

Rnd 3: Knit.

Rnd 4: Purl.

Rnd 5: Bind off knitwise. Break yarn. Weave in ends and block.

And Toto Too?

A simple beanie with a simple color pattern. The crown decreases spiral the color work into a tornado design.

Size
One size

Finished Measurements
Circumference 20 inches / 50.75 cm

Height to crown 7.25 inches / 18.5 cm

Total height 8.75 inches / 22.25 cm

Materials
Schoolhouse Press Unspun (Icelandic 100% Unspun Wool; 300 yds per 3.5 oz wheel); MC; Beige 1 wheel. CC: Dusty Pink 1 wheel.

US#6 / 4.25 mm needles, or two sizes smaller than size needed to obtain gauge

US#8/ 5 mm needles, configured for circular knitting, or size needed to obtain gauge.

Large-eyed sewing needle

Stitch marker

Gauge
18 sts and 24 rounds = 4 inches / 10 cm in color pattern

Special Instructions
Two color cast on

Using MC as the yarn that goes over the needle, and CC as the yarn that wraps around the thumb and traps the stitch, work long tail cast on.

Pattern
With smaller needle, and using two color cast on method, cast on 90 sts. Leave a 12 inch / 30.5 cm end for seaming later.

Rows 1 and 2: With MC, knit.

Rows 3 and 4: With CC, knit.

Change to larger needle, and join to work in the round, placing a marker for beginning of round.

Work all rnds of And Toto Too? Main Chart.

Decrease top

Work And Toto Too? decrease chart. Use ssk for the decrease in the color designated on chart.

Finishing

Break yarn, leaving a 12 inch / 30.5 cm end. Thread yarn needle. Work yarn needle through remaining sts. Pull taut to close top of hat. Weave in ends.

Neatly seam garter st band with tails from the cast on.

Block.

 No stitch

MC

CC

Ssk

Crown Chart

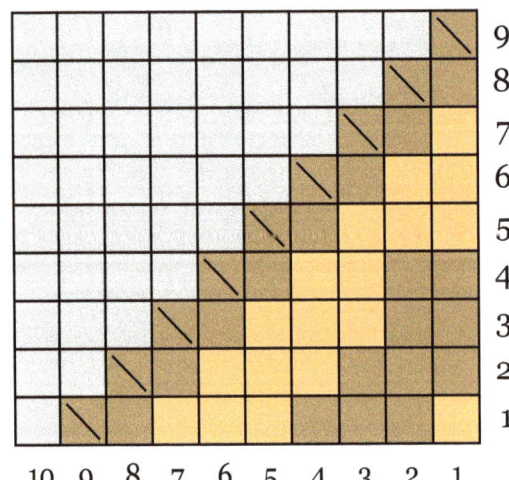

Main Chart

Eastern Light

The color work on this hat is a traditional design incorporating crosses and diamonds. The crown shaping yields a surprisingly asymmetrical design.

Size
One size

Finished Measurements
Circumference 21.25 inches / 54 cm

Height to crown 6.75 inches / 17.25 cm

Total height 8.5 inches / 21.5 cm

Materials
Schoolhouse Press Unspun Icelandic (100% Unspun Wool; 300 yds per 3.5 oz wheel); MC; Blacksheep 1 wheel. CC: Sumac 1 wheel.

US#6 / 4.25 mm needles, or two sizes smaller than size needed to obtain gauge

US#8/ 5 mm needles, configured for circular knitting, or size needed to obtain gauge.

Large-eyed sewing needle

Stitch marker

Gauge
18 sts and 26 rounds = 4 inches / 10 cm in color pattern

Special Instructions
Two color cast on

Using MC as the yarn that goes over the needle, and CC as the yarn that wraps around the thumb and traps the stitch, work long tail cast on.

Pattern
With smaller needles, and using the two color cast on method, cast on 96 sts. Being careful not to twist, join to work in the round, placing a marker at the beginning of the rnd.

Rnds 1 - 5: Work first 5 rnds of Eastern Light chart.

Change to larger needles. Continuing following chart through crown decrease. Use ssk for the decrease in the color designated on the chart.

Finishing

Break yarn, leaving a 12 inch / 30.5 cm end. Thread yarn needle. Work yarn needle through remaining sts. Pull taut to close top of hat and weave in ends and block.

	No stitch
	MC
	CC
•	Purl
◣	Ssk

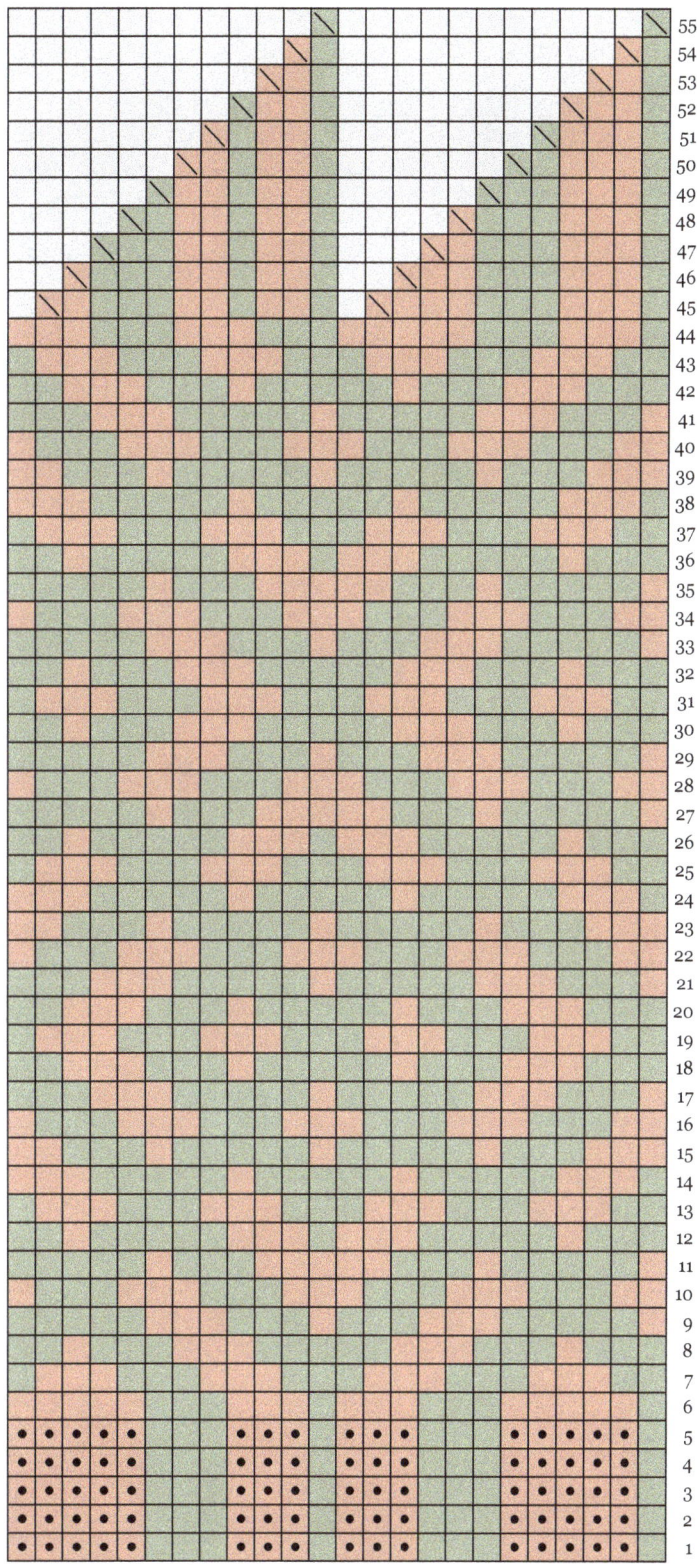

Electric Cloche

This hat is a sweet little cloche with two color purl bump textured stripes. The asymmetry of the striping adds to the fun. This design would work well with short remnants in your stash. No need for any of the stripes to match!

Sizes
S (M, L, 1X)

Finished Measurements
Circumference 17.75 (19.5, 21.25, 23) inches / 45 (49.5, 54, 58.5) cm

Height to crown 8.75 inches

Total height 10 (10.25, 10.5, 10.75) inches

Materials
Schoolhouse Press Unspun Icelandic (100% Un-Spun Wool; 300 yds per 3.5 oz wheel); MC; Sumac 1 wheel. CC1: Black Sheep, CC2: Lake Blue, CC3: Wood Violet, CC4: Shocking Pink, approximately 80 yds of each color

US#8/ 5 mm needles, configured for circular knitting, or size needed to obtain gauge.

Large-eyed sewing needle

Stitch marker

Gauge
18 sts and 24 rounds = 4 inches / 10 cm in pattern stitch

Pattern Notes
In order to maintain the integrity of the design, the height to the crown is the same for all of the different sizes of this hat. Consequently, the smaller sizes will be a more slouchy hat than the larger sizes. You can adapt the pattern by removing a stripe or two of your choice to make the hat shorter. You can also remove a rnd between the stripes to shorten the height. Conversely, you could add stripes or rnds between the stripes to lengthen the height. Play with it. No matter what you decide, the resulting hat will be aesthetically pleasing.

Pattern
With MC, cast on 80 (88, 96, 104) sts. Being careful not to twist, join to work in the round, placing a marker at the beginning of the rnd.

Rnds 1 - 5: Knit.

Rnd 6: With CC1, knit.

Rnd 7: With CC2, *p2tog; repeat to end of rnd.

Rnd 8: With CC1, *kfb; repeat to end of rnd.

Break CC1 and CC2.

Rnds 9 - 14: With MC, knit.

Rnds 15 - 17: Repeat Rnds 6 - 8.

Rnds 18 - 20: With MC, knit.

Rnds 21 - 23: Repeat Rnds 6 - 8.

Rnds 24 - 26: With MC, knit.

Rnd 27: With CC3, knit.

Rnd 28: With CC4, *p2tog; repeat from * to end of rnd.

Rnd 29: With CC3, *kfb; repeat from * to end of rnd.

Break CC3 and CC4.

Rnds 30 - 32: With MC, knit.

Rnds 33 - 35: Repeat Rnds 27 - 29.

Rnds 36 - 38: With MC, knit.

Rnds 39 - 41: Repeat Rnds 27 - 29.

Rnds 42 - 44: With MC, knit.

Rnds 45 - 47: Repeat Rnds 6 - 8.

Rnds 48 - 52: With MC, knit.

Decrease top

Size 1X only: *K11, ssk; repeat from * to end of rnd. 96 sts.

Sizes L (1X) only: *K10, ssk; repeat from * to end of rnd. 88 sts.

Size M (L, 1X) only: *K9, ssk; repeat from * to end of rnd. 80 sts.

All sizes

Rnd 1: *K8 ssk; repeat from * to end of rnd. 72 sts.

Rnd 2: *K7 ssk; repeat from * to end of rnd. 64 sts.

Rnd 3: *K6 ssk; repeat from * to

end of rnd. 56 sts

Rnd 4: *K5 ssk; repeat from * to end of rnd. 48 sts.

Rnd 5: *K4 ssk; repeat from * to end of rnd. 40 sts.

Rnd 6: *K3 ssk; repeat from * to end of rnd. 32 sts.

Rnd 7: *K2 ssk; repeat from * to end of rnd. 24 sts.

Rnd 8: *K1 ssk; repeat from * to end of rnd. 16 sts

Rnd 9: *Ssk; repeat from * to end of rnd. 8 sts.

Finishing

Break yarn, leaving a 12 inch / 30.5 cm end. Thread yarn needle. Work yarn needle through remaining sts. Pull taut to close top of hat. Weave in ends.

Block.

Sweet Peerie

The color work on this hat uses simple Peerie patterns that have a lovely rhythm when knit. Try using highly contrasting colors or a gradient dyed yarn for the contrasting color for a different effect.

Sizes
XS (S, M, L)

Finished Measurements
Circumference 16.75 (18.75, 20, 21.5) inches /

Height to crown (excluding earflap) 5 (6, 7.5, 8.5) inches / 12.75 (15.25, 19, 21.75) cm

Total height (excluding earflap) 7 (8, 9.5, 10.5) inches / 17.75 (20.25, 24, 26.5) cm

Materials
Schoolhouse Press Unspun Icelandic (100% Un-Spun Wool; 300 yds per 3.5 oz wheel); MC; Sumac 1 wheel. CC1: Dark Caramel, CC2: Cayenne, CC3: Gold, approximately 100 yds of each color

US#8/ 5 mm needles, configured for circular knitting, or size needed to obtain gauge.

Large-eyed sewing needle

Stitch marker

Gauge
18 sts and 24 rounds = 4 inches / 10 cm in pattern stitch

Pattern
Ear flap (Make 2)

With MC, cast on 2 sts, leaving a yard long end for braiding later. Working back and forth, following Ear Flap Chart, adding colors as indicated.

Join for hat

With MC, knit across 20 sts on one ear flap, cast on 24 (26, 30, 34) sts, knit across 20 sts on second ear flap, cast on 12 (18, 20, 22) sts. 76 (84, 90, 96) sts. Join to work in the round. Place marker to denote beginning of round.

Rnd 1: K20 , p 24 (26, 30, 34) sts, k20, p12 (18, 20, 22) sts.

Work 29 (34, 45, 45) rnds of Sweet Peerie Chart around. For L size only, repeat rnds 14-18.

Next rnd: With MC, knit, decreasing 6 (4, 0, 6) sts evenly. 70 (80, 90, 90) sts.

Decrease top

Rnd 1: *K8, k2tog; repeat from * to end of rnd. 63 (72, 81, 81) sts.

Rnd 2: *K7, k2tog; repeat from * to end of rnd. 56 (64, 72, 72) sts.

Rnd 3: *K6, k2tog; repeat from * to end of rnd. 49 (56, 63, 63) sts.

Rnd 4: *K5, k2tog; repeat from * to end of rnd. 42 (48, 54, 54) sts.

Rnd 5: *K4, k2tog; repeat from * to end of rnd. 35 (40, 45, 45) sts.

Rnd 6: *K3, k2tog; repeat from * to end of rnd. 28 (32, 36, 36) sts.

Rnd 7: *K2, k2tog]; repeat from * to end of rnd. 21 (24, 27, 27) sts.

Rnd 8: *K1, k2tog; repeat from * to end of rnd. 14 (16, 18, 18) sts.

Rnd 9: *K2tog; repeat from * to end of rnd. 7 (8, 9, 9) sts.

Finishing

Break yarn, leaving a 12 inch / 30.5 cm end. Thread yarn needle. Work yarn needle through remaining sts. Pull taut to close top of hat. Weave in ends.

Cut two 36 inch lengths of each color of yarn. With sewing needle, draw each length through the bottom of one ear flap. Match ends so that the ear flap is in the middle of the length of yarn. Divide yarn into three sections of three and braid.

When braid is 12 - 14 inches long, or desired length tie the end with an over hand knot and trim the ends. Repeat with the other ear flap, then block.

Earflap Chart

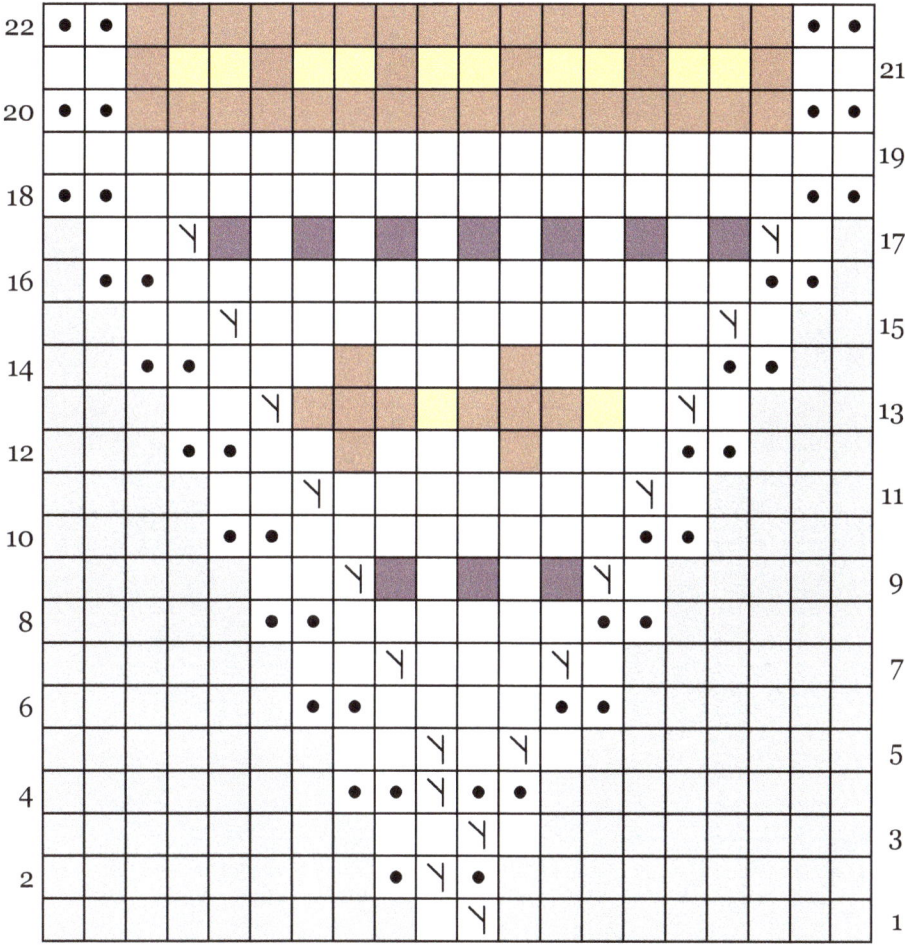

Main Chart

				45
				44
CC1		CC1		43
				42
				41
CC3		CC3		40
CC2	CC3	CC2	CC3	39
CC3	CC3	CC3	CC3	38
				37
				36
CC1		CC1		35
				34
				33
CC3	CC3			32
CC2	CC3	CC3	CC2	31
		CC3		30
				29
				28
CC1		CC1		27
				26
				25
CC3	CC3	CC3		24
CC3	CC2	CC3		23
CC3	CC3	CC3		22
				21
				20
CC1		CC1		19
				18
				17
			CC3	16
CC2	CC2	CC3	CC3	15
	CC3	CC3	CC3	14
				13
				12
CC1		CC1		11
				10
				9
CC3	CC3	CC3		8
	CC3	CC3		7
CC3	CC2	CC2	CC3	6
	CC3	CC3		5
CC3		CC3		4
				3
				2
	CC1	CC1		1

4 3 2 1

Legend

- ☐ No stitch
- ☐ MC
- ■ CC1
- ☐ CC2
- ■ CC3
- Y Kfb
- • Purl

132

Eastern Diamonds

Here is another take on the traditional pattern used in Eastern Light. This time the large motif is centered and the background is filled with diamonds. The hat is decreased at ten points resulting in an asymmetrical design on the crown.If I were to knit it again, I'd play with the crown design a bit; maybe incorporating the diamonds into the crown instead. But I love the design on the rest of the hat.

Size
One size

Finished Measurements
Circumference 22 inches / 55.75 cm

Total height 9 inches / 22.75 cm

Materials
Schoolhouse Press Unspun Icelandic (100% Unspun Woo; 300 yds per 3.5 oz wheel); MC; Wood Violet 1 wheel. CC: Winter Blue 1 wheel.

US#6/ 4 mm needles, configured for circular knitting, or 2 sizes smaller than larger needle

US#8/ 5 mm needles, configured for circular knitting, or size needed to obtain gauge

Large-eyed sewing needle

Stitch marker

Gauge
18 sts and 24 rounds = 4 inches / 10 cm in color pattern

Special Instructions
Two color cast on

Using MC as the yarn that goes over the needle, and CC as the yarn that wraps around the thumb and traps the stitch, work long tail cast on.

Pattern
With smaller needles, and using two color cast on method, cast on 100 sts. Leave a 12 inch / 30.5 cm end for sewing up later.

Rows 1 - 4: With MC, knit.

Rows 5 - 6: With CC, knit.

Rows 7 - 8: With MC, knit.

Change to larger needles, and join to work in the round, placing a marker at the beginning of the round.

Work all 56 rnds of Eastern Diamonds chart, using ssk for your decrease in the color specified.

▨	No stitch
☐	MC
▨	CC
◺	Ssk

Finishing

Break yarn, leaving a 12 inch / 30.5 cm end. Thread yarn needle. Work yarn needle through remaining sts. Pull taut to close top of hat.

Using CO tail, neatly seam garter st band. Weave in ends.

Block.

Le Plat

A beret! The easy color work pattern repeats and then changes after decreasing for the top. It's a simple change that keeps the knitting interesting. Block it over a plate to achieve the beret shape or wear it as a slouch hat. This design can also be knit in a heavy Aran or bulky weight yarn.

Sizes
S (M, L, 1X)

Finished Measurements
Circumference 18 (20.25, 22, 23.5) inches /

Height to crown 6 (7.5, 7.5, 9.5) inches / 15.25 (19, 19, 24) cm

Total height 9 (11, 11, 13) inches / 22.75 (28, 28, 33) cm

Materials
Schoolhouse Press Unspun Icelandic (100% Un-Spun Wool; 300 yds per 3.5 oz wheel); MC; Dusty Pink 1 wheel. CC1: Wood Violet, CC2: Shocking Pink, approximately 100 yds of each color

US#6/ 4 mm needles, configured for circular knitting, or 2 sizes smaller than larger needle

US#8/ 5 mm needles, configured for circular knitting, or size needed to obtain gauge

Large-eyed sewing needle

Stitch marker

Gauge
15 sts and 19 rounds = 4 inches / 10 cm in pattern stitch

14 sts and 19 rounds = 4 inches / 10 cm in rib stitch

Pattern
Work with two strands of Unspun, held double, throughout.

With MC and smaller needles, cast on 68 (76, 82, 88) sts. Being careful not to twist, join to work in the round. Place marker at the beginning of the rnd.

Rnds 1 - 12: *K1, p1; repeat from * to end of rnd.

Change to larger needles.

Rnd 13: Knit, increasing 16 (14, 14, 14) sts in next rnd. 84 (90, 96, 102) sts.

Work Chart A attaching CC1 and CC2 as indicated.

Work Chart A a total of 2 (3, 3, 3) times 20 (30, 30, 30) rnds.

Break CC1 and CC2, and continue with MC only.

Decrease Rnd 1: *K1, k2tog; repeat from * to end of end. 56 (60, 64, 68) sts.

Decrease Rnd 2: Knit.

Work Chart B, attaching CC1 and CC2 as indicated.

Break CC1 and CC2, and continue with MC only.

Decrease Rnd 3: *K2tog; repeat from * to end of rnd. 28 (30, 32, 34) sts.

Decrease Rnd 4: Knit.

Decrease Rnd 5: *K2tog; repeat from * to end of rnd. 14 (15, 16, 17) sts.

Finishing

Break yarn, leaving a 12 inch / 30.5 cm end. Thread yarn needle. Work yarn needle through remaining sts. Pull taut to close top of hat. Weave in ends.

Block.

To shape as a beret: Soak hat in cool water for a few hours or over-night. Gently squeeze out excess water and stretch hat across a 10-12 inch dinner plate. Center pattern on plate. Stand ribbing up. Allow to dry completely before removing.

Chart A

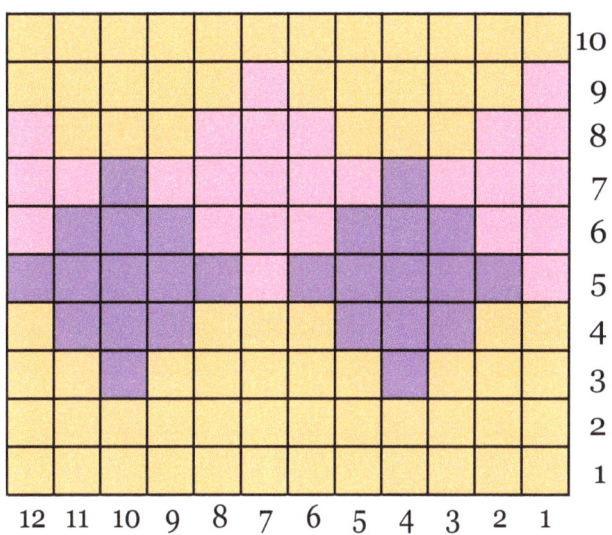

Chart B

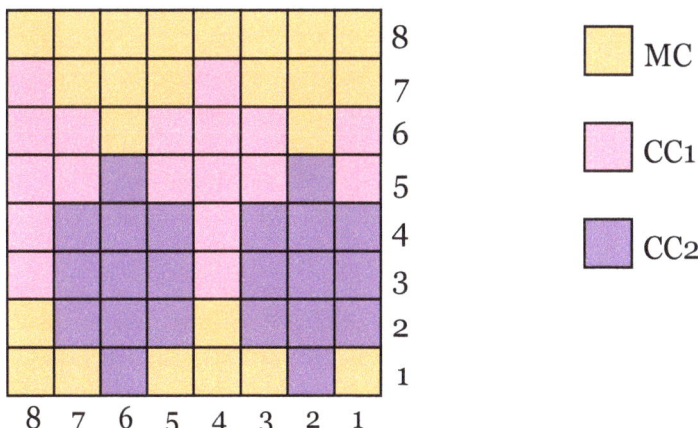

MC

CC1

CC2

Epilogue

From the blog:

I love the week between Christmas and New Year's Day. In my little world, it is always the most relaxing week of the year. The Christmas frenzy is over and everyone is pre-occupied with football. The world seems to slow down during this time, spinning so slowly that we rarely see the sun.

From a knitting perspective, This was an exceptionally good year. I challenged myself to knit 30 hats in 30 days and I did! But I could not have done it without support and encouragement from family and friends.

I learned a few things too.

Knitting is so much quicker when you have a plan. The more complicated hats were easier to knit because everything was planned before I started. The plain hats took much longer because I was making decisions on the fly and often had to rip back and try again.

It's easier to knit a hat when you don't have a particular head in mind. I'm always overly concerned about the fit when I'm knitting for someone specific. Surprisingly, each hat fit all sorts of heads in all sorts of sizes.

Blogging everyday is practically impossible for me. Even if I have the time, the desire is not there. It's difficult to stay fresh. But it's also difficult to start blogging again when I've been away for a while.

I have more ideas stored in my head than I thought. I was surprised how one idea led to another. I didn't even get to use ideas that I had in the beginning.

It was a fun challenge but other challenges await. I wonder what they'll be.

Abbreviations

1/2 LC: Slip 1 st to cn, hold in front, k2, k1 from cn
1/2 RC: Slip 2 sts to cn, hold in back, k1, k2 from cn
1/3LC: Slip 1 st to cn, hold in front, k3, k1 from can
2/2 LC: Slip 2 sts to cn, hold in back, k2, k2 from cn
2/2 RC: Slip 2 sts to cn, hold in front, k2, k2 from cn
3/1RC: Slip 3 sts to cn, hold in back, k1, k3 from can
5/5 LC: Slip 4 sts to cn, hold in front, k5, k4 from can
5/5RC: Slip 5 sts to cn, hold in back, k4, k5 from cn
CC - contrast color
cn - cable needle
k - knit
k2tog - knit 2 sts together
k3tog - knit 3 sts together
kfb - knit into front and back of next st
MC - main color
p - purl
p2tog - purl 2 sts together
p3tog - purl 3 sts together
rnd(s) - round(s)
s2kp - slip 2 sts knitwise, k1, pass 2 slipped sts over
ssk - slip, slip, knit
st(s) - stitch(es)
yo - yarn over

Sources

Adriafil Sri
Rimini, Italy
adriafil.com

Blackberry Ridge Woolen Mill
3776 Forshaug Road
Mt. Horeb, WI 53572
USA
blackberry-ridge.com

Knit One Crochet Too
Fort Myers, FL
USA
knitonecrochettoo.com

Lang Yarns
Reiden, Switzerland
langyarns.com

Noro Yarns
Knitting Fever Inc.
Long Island NY
USA
knittingfever.com

Schachenmayr
SirdarUSA
406 20th Street SE
Hickory, NC
USA
schachenmayr.com

Schoolhouse Press
6899 Cary Bluff
Pittsville, WI 54466
USA
schoolhousepress.com

Universal Yarn
5991 Caldwell Business Park
Drive
Harrisburg, NC 28075
USA
universalyarn.com

Acknowledgments

Thanks to the staff of Cooperative Press, especially Shannon Okey for her inspiration and confidence, and to Andi Smith for her expert technical assistance, feedback and encouragement.

Thanks to all my cheerleaders during the 30 days, especially Marilyn Shwarz, Jennifer Fox, Jennifer Riester, Nancy Whitinger, Amy Peacock Smith, and my sister, Elaine Deslauriers.

And thanks to my knitting friends, especially Ann Swanson, Sue Dempsey, Lynn Shannon, and Deanna Pooler for their advice and encouragement.

About Marie

Marie Duquette has been a daily knitter since childhood. She lives in Madison Wisconsin with her family.

Since retiring from her work as an advocate for people with developmental health challenges, she has been devoting more time to designing. She can be found on social media as Wool Forward.

Marie can be found on

Facebook: http://www.facebook.com/cooperativepress
Instagram: http://www.instagram.com/cooperativepress
Ravelry: http://www.ravelry.com/people/cooperativepress
Web/shop: http://cooperativepress.com

About CP

Cooperative Press was founded in 2007 by Shannon Okey. She had been doing freelance acquisitions work, introducing authors with projects she believed in to editors at various publishers. And although working with traditional publishers can be very rewarding, there are some books that fly under their radar. They're too avant-garde, or the marketing department doesn't know how to sell them, or they don't think they'll sell 50,000 copies in a year.

5,000 or 50,000. Does the book matter to that 5,000? Then it should be published.

In 2009, Cooperative Press (cooperativepress. com) changed its name to reflect the relationships we have developed with authors working on books. We work together to put out the best quality books we can and share in the proceeds accordingly.

Thank you for supporting independent publishers and authors.

Cooperative Press can be found on

Facebook: http://www.facebook.com/cooperativepress
Instagram: http://www.instagram.com/cooperativepress
Ravelry: http://www.ravelry.com/people/cooperativepress
Web/shop: http://cooperativepress.com

CPSIA information can be obtained
at www.ICGtesting.com
Printed in the USA
BVHW090023111019
560795BV00009BA/50/P